Loving Lindsey

Patricia Keelyn

Panther Press

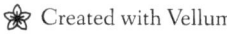 Created with Vellum

This one's for Penny Kelly, Pam Koviak, Sharyn Kloster, and Susan Van Wie.
Sisters extraordinaire and good friends all.

Table of Contents

Connections

Welcome to The Protectors Series.

This is a "themed" series where each book stands alone but with a common element. All the heroes are ex-military, who see themselves as protectors for the people in their lives. All five books are romantic suspense, but some are more intense, edgier, with more focus on the suspense than others.

There are, however, two other connections in these books. Two of them, Loving Lindsey and Becca and the Beast, take place in the same small town, Willowbend Wyoming, and they have common characters. Also, the hero in Nobody's Hero appears in one of my Mother's Heart Books, Keeping Katie. I guess there are just some characters and places I can't let go of.

Enjoy, Pat Lewin

Chapter One

Will Claxton could smell trouble brewing a mile away, but tonight he didn't need to go that far. Seated on his favorite bar stool at The Rusty Spur, a run-down watering hole on the outskirts of Willow-bend, Wyoming, the place was primed and ready.

Winter had released its hold on the land, and it seemed nearly every cowhand in the county felt the urge to shake off the doldrums of the long cold months. And they'd picked the Spur to do it. The smoke, the tinny music spewing from the jukebox, the crack and drop of pool balls, and the raucous laughter of beer-guzzling cowboys spelled a fight just waiting to happen. Sooner or later, some drunk would take exception to another's looks or brand, and that would set things off.

Will figured it was time to finish his beer and call it a night. Before all hell broke loose.

Then the front door opened, letting in a blast of chilly spring air. And in walked a familiar figure. Tall, slender, and dressed in work-worn jeans and boots with a hat pulled low over her eyes, she looked more like a young saddle hand than a woman, a saddle hand itching for a fight.

She whipped off her hat, slapping it against one slender thigh, and all resemblance to a cowboy flew out the door. She was all female, from her wild mane of reddish-blond hair, to the feminine curves accentuated by no-nonsense cotton and denim.

Lindsey Baker.

He remembered the last time he'd seen her and that it had struck him then too: the differences between the girl he'd once known—a lanky tomboy trailing behind him—and the woman she'd become. Yes sir, Lindsey could pretend she was one of the guys, had done so all her life in fact, but any man with half an eye could see differently.

"Damn," muttered Eric, the bartender.

Will couldn't have agreed more. Though he would have bet Eric's definition of trouble differed somewhat from his own. Lindsey had always been one of the most difficult females Will knew, and he suspected *that* much about her hadn't changed.

"What the hell is she doing here?" Will asked.

Frowning, Eric nodded toward the back of the room. "I suspect she's looking for her brother."

Will followed the other man's gaze to a threesome involved in a pool game. Two of the men he'd never seen before. The third he'd known all his life—Stuart, Lindsey's younger brother. Will had noticed the younger Baker earlier and purposely steered clear of him. "And the strangers?"

"Drifters," Eric answered, though he kept his focus on the impending confrontation. "They blew into town a couple of weeks ago. Been hustling the local cowboys ever since. Baker more than most. Boy's been losing his shirt."

Eric shook his head. "As if his sister needs any more trouble right now."

Will glanced at Eric. *"More* trouble?"

"Seems she's run into a string of bad luck out on the Silver Creek. Accidents and the like. A lot of the boys won't work for her anymore."

Will had heard about the so-called problems out on the Baker ranch but had dismissed them as hearsay. Around these parts, rumors traveled like wildfire across a dry summer prairie, and when it came to the Bakers, folks tended to keep Will informed, whether he was interested or not. Eric, however, wasn't one to spread tales, and his information was usually more accurate than most.

Making a mental note to find out more later, Will took another sip of his beer and watched Lindsey's progress across the room. Men shifted out of her way and fell silent as she walked toward her brother. Will had to admire the way she carried herself with a smooth feminine confidence that contradicted her situation. She might have been a woman out of place in a raunchy cowboy bar, but it didn't stop her. But then, nothing much ever had. In grade school, she'd been the toughest "boy" on the playground. Now she ran one of the largest spreads in the area.

He doubted whether any of the locals would mess with her. They all knew Lindsey and her reputation. But the men with Stuart—well, that was another story. There was no telling what a couple of rough-looking strangers like those two might do.

Finishing the last of his beer, Will told himself it wasn't his problem. He didn't owe the Bakers anything. Hell, a lot of folks would say it was the other way around. Besides, Lindsey knew better than to come waltzing into the Spur. If she got herself into trouble, it was no concern of his.

"Stuart?" Her voice carried across the room, and the hum of conversation died. "We need to talk."

Stu didn't seem to notice that every eye in the place was on the two of them. "Not now, Sis, I'm in the middle of a game." With a grin, he leaned over the table to line up a shot. "These boys been on a winning streak, and I mean to turn that around."

The two men laughed, but Lindsey didn't look amused.

Stu took the shot and missed. "Damn!"

The other two players groaned in mock sympathy, and several of the cowboys closest to the table laughed nervously.

"There, see . . ." Stu walked over to his sister and draped an arm around her shoulder. "You went and caused me to miss."

She said something Will couldn't hear, but he sensed her tension from clear across the room. She was one unhappy woman. Stu, on the other hand, didn't seem to notice. Either that, or he didn't care.

"Hey, guys," Stuart said. "I want you to meet my big sister Lindsey." He put a hand under her chin which she batted away. Chuckling, he pulled her closer against his side. "She may not be the fanciest filly in these parts, but she's got spunk. And she can run a ranch better than any man I know. Ain't that right, Linds?"

"Damn fool," Will muttered. He and Lindsey might not be on the best of terms, but he hated seeing her humiliated —especially by her no-account brother.

Lindsey pulled away, ignoring her brother's comments. "Playtime's over, Stuart. Tomorrow's branding day, and I need you sober and able to work. Let's go."

"I can't. We're in the middle—"

Lindsey didn't let him finish. "Not anymore." Moving

over to the table, she swept the remaining balls into the pockets. "The game's over."

Will almost laughed aloud. No one could say the woman didn't have guts.

Stu and his new friends, however, weren't smiling. The bigger of the two strangers stepped in front of her, stopping her as she turned toward the door. "Hey, missy. Where ya think you're goin'?"

Lindsey lifted her chin and looked him in the eye. "Stay out of this, cowboy. It's between me and my brother."

He dropped two meaty hands to his hips. "You just messed up our game. That makes it 'tween you and me."

Stuart came to his sister's defense. "Hey, Gus. Take it easy, buddy. Lindsey's hot-tempered, but she didn't mean nothin' by it. Did ya, Sis?"

"Sure I did, *Gus.*" Lindsey never took her eyes off the big man in front of her. "You and your friend are nothing but a couple of two-bit hustlers. Now get out of my way. My brother and I are leaving."

Will groaned. Gutsy maybe, but stupid. Very stupid.

"Your brother here owes us. Big time. And you aren't goin' anywhere till he pays up." Gus shifted in closer, obviously trying to intimidate her with his size.

Will could have told the man it wouldn't work. He'd never known Lindsey to back down from anything in her life. And as he expected, she didn't even flinch. "Get out of my way."

"Not likely. But maybe we can work out some other form of payment." Gus seized her arm and hauled her up against his chest.

Without thinking, Will unhooked his feet from the barstool and started to stand.

"Get your hands off me." Anger, not fear, echoed in Lindsey's voice, and it brought Will up short.

What the hell was he doing?

Lindsey wasn't his responsibility. Never had been, really. They'd been friends, but it had been a long time ago. Forcing himself to sit back down, he decided to let Stuart get her out of this one. After all, *he* was her brother.

As if hearing Will's thoughts, Stu grabbed the big man's arm. "Leave her be, Gus. I'll pay you."

"I think I might like her form of payment better. What do you think, Ray?" Gus said to his partner. "'Neath these cowboy duds, I feel a woman."

Stu yanked at Gus's arm just as Ray, a small weasel of a man, stepped into the fray. He gripped Stu by the shoulder and spun him around. Before he could react, Ray buried a fist in Stu's stomach, followed by an uppercut to his jaw. Stu collapsed on the floor.

Lindsey let out an angry curse and rammed her knee upward, aiming for Gus's groin.

Gus blocked it and laughed. "Looks like I got me a wildcat."

"Damn!" Will knew better than to get involved—just like the rest of the cowboys, who shifted uncomfortably, but did nothing while one of their own lay crumpled on the floor. Hell, why did he have to be the one to step forward?

Especially when it involved the Bakers.

"Damn," he mumbled again as he reached the gathering around the pool table. He might not like it, but he knew the answer to his own question. He couldn't stand by and watch someone manhandle a woman. Not even if that woman was Jeremiah Baker's daughter.

"Got a problem here, Lindsey?" he asked.

Her gaze jumped to his, and he saw the surprise in

those bright green eyes of hers. He couldn't blame her. She probably figured he'd be the last one to come to her rescue, but it was too late now to worry about what Lindsey thought.

"You best just go on back to the bar," Gus said. "This ain't none of your concern."

Will crossed his arms and rested a hip against one corner of the pool table, sizing up the other man with a glance. He was too damn big.

"Well, you see, Gus, it's like this." Will figured he'd done stupider things in his life. Only at the moment, he couldn't think of one. "Miss Baker here and I go back a ways. Since she took a swing at me in the first grade to be exact." He rubbed his jaw, as if remembering that long-ago punch. "I figure that makes her my concern."

Gus sneered, turning his plain face ugly. "Sounds like it's time someone taught her some manners."

"It isn't going to be you." Will paused to let his words sink in. "Now. Let the lady—"

"Will," Lindsey called out, looking at something behind him. "Watch out!"

Spinning around, Will came face to face with Gus's sidekick, the man called Ray. Will braced himself, ready for the attack, when suddenly Eric emerged from the crowd, close to Ray's back and whispered something in the man's ear.

The drifter stopped in his tracks.

Imagining Eric's threat, Will grinned and nodded his thanks before turning back to Gus. "As I said, let the lady go."

Gus's eyes flickered briefly with uncertainty but then hardened. He shoved Lindsey away from him, and she caught hold of the pool table to keep from falling.

"Okay," Gus said. Legs braced slightly apart, hands at his side, he wiggled his fingers in a come-and-get-me gesture. "You want to be a hero? Go for it."

Gus stood a good two or three inches taller than Will's six feet. Add to that about a hundred pounds, and Will figured he didn't stand a chance in a fair fight. But then, who said he had to fight fair? One thing eight years in the marines had taught him: things weren't always fair. In the end, the only thing that mattered was who was left standing.

"Hell . . ." Will crossed his arms as if reconsidering. "Looks like I don't stand a chance against the likes of you."

Gus chuckled, a low, mean sound. "You got that right."

Will dropped his hands, started to turn away, but then grabbed a pool cue instead. In one fluid motion, he brought the hard wooden stick around and caught old Gus in the gut. A quick uppercut to his chin with an elbow, and then Will swept the man's knees with the pool cue.

He fell hard.

Lindsey let out her breath as Gus hit the floor. She'd seen men like him before—big, mean, and unpredictable. Fortunately, Will's move had been a surprise, or else he might have been in trouble. Obviously, she should have known better than to worry. Will had always been able to take care of himself.

Planting one booted foot on Gus's chest, Will leveled the pointed end of the cue at the other man's throat. "Now, what was that you were saying about manners?"

Gus cursed but quieted at the distinctive sound of a pump-action shotgun. Like everyone else in the room, Lindsey turned toward Eric as he stepped forward, weapon in hand, shoving Gus's partner in front of him.

"Nothing like a good old-fashioned fistfight to liven up

the evening." Eric grinned at the roomful of cowboys. "But now"—he motioned with the shotgun for Gus to stand—"I think it's time you two boys moved on."

Will lifted his boot from Gus's chest and stepped back.

Scrambling to his feet, Gus glared at Will before shooting a poisonous glance at Lindsey. "You ain't heard the last of me."

A sliver of fear slipped down her spine, but she refused to acknowledge it. Lifting her chin, she returned his angry gaze.

"Oh, I think we have." Eric's words broke the uncomfortable connection. "At least in my place." He stood with his shotgun draped across one arm in a gesture that was about as casual as a rattler ready to strike. "In fact, either of you boys walk through that door again, it won't be me doing the talking."

Gus hesitated a moment longer, then turning, he led the way as both men hurried toward the exit. As soon as the door slammed behind them, the noise level returned to normal.

Lindsey could hardly believe how quickly everyone went back to their own business, as if nothing had happened. Shaking her head at the strange workings of the male mind, she turned to her brother. He was attempting to stand, and she slipped an arm around his waist to help him.

"Is he okay?" Will asked.

"He'll live." She got Stuart to his feet but had to brace him against the wall to keep him from slipping back to the floor. The combination of too much beer and the blow to his jaw made him nearly useless.

"What about you?"

Surprised, she glanced at Will. The concern in his dark eyes made her heart skip a beat. She wasn't used to anyone asking about her well-being, but then, Will wasn't most people. He'd once been her best friend.

"I'm fine," she lied.

"Sure?"

She didn't answer for a moment. Why did it have to be Will who'd come to her defense tonight? He'd always been able to unnerve her with little more than a glance. Now he stood too close, looking at her as if he cared, as if *she* mattered to him, when she knew nothing could be further from the truth.

"I'm fine," she repeated.

He didn't look like he believed her, but he let it go. "Here . . ." He moved to Stuart's side. "Let me help."

"No, thanks." He'd done enough already, more than she would have liked. She'd come into The Rusty Spur angry and determined to drag her brother back to the ranch. Instead, Stuart had ended up hurt, and she'd gotten herself manhandled by some big oaf. The whole incident embarrassed her, but Will witnessing it and coming to her rescue made it even worse. "We'll manage."

"Just like you managed Gus?" It was a typical Will statement, ripe with sarcasm.

She'd forgotten this particular trait of his. He'd always been so damned cocky and sure of himself. She would have liked to tell him to take a walk, but she held her tongue. She didn't want another scene. And besides, he *had* helped her.

Smiling tightly, she stepped away from Stuart. "Be my guest."

Will slipped a shoulder under Stuart's arm and started toward the exit. He waited until they were almost to the door before starting in on her.

"What were you thinking, coming in here alone like

that?" he asked. "Why didn't you send a ranch hand in for Stu?"

She should have known he wouldn't just help her out the door and leave it at that. "I handle my own problems, Will."

"I noticed."

She turned back toward him. She had enough on her mind between the troubles on the ranch and Stuart's irrational behavior. The last thing she needed was a lecture from Will Claxton. "No one asked you to step in."

For a moment, he held her gaze, and she saw the old anger flare in his eyes. The same anger she'd seen the last time they'd argued, the night their friendship had ended.

"That's right," he said finally. "No one did."

It took her back a bit: his brief flash of anger and the memories it stirred. For years, she'd avoided him, and now she realized why. She didn't want to be reminded of the friendship they'd once shared, or the night it had ended.

"I appreciate the help, Will. But Stuart and I can manage from here."

"Gus and his pal might still be around."

She tried to smile, but doubted she'd succeeded. "We'll be fine."

Keeping his hold on Stu, Will ignored her and started again toward the door. Lindsey had no choice but to go along, knowing just how stubborn Will could be once he'd set his mind on something. And how useless it was to oppose him.

Outside, it took both of them to get Stuart into the truck. Once they had, she turned back to Will. "Well, I guess I owe you."

He slipped his hands into the back pockets of his jeans and smiled. "Yeah, I guess you do at that."

"Thank you." Though it nearly killed her to say it. "I always pay my debts. So, if there's anything I can do . . ." She let her voice trail off and turned toward her truck, eager to get away from him.

"In fact," Will said, stopping her before she'd taken three steps. "There is something you can do for me."

She turned, eyeing him suspiciously. Something in his voice made her wary. "What's that?"

"You have something that belongs to me."

"I don't know what you're talking about."

"Don't you?"

She shook her head. "Look, Will—"

"The Claxton Ranch." He closed the distance between them. "I think it's about time the Bakers returned what they stole."

Chapter Two

"Stole!" Lindsey took a step backward, and just as quickly cursed herself for doing so. "My father claimed that land legally."

"Oh, it was legal all right." Will crossed his arms and frowned. "But just because something's legal doesn't make it right."

Heat brushed her cheeks, and Lindsey thanked heaven for the darkness. She agreed with him, and though she'd never told him, she'd argued his case with her father at the time. It hadn't made any difference. Jeremiah Baker had wanted the Claxton property, and he'd taken it.

Will stepped toward her, jarring her back to the uncomfortable reality that she was standing too close to him. "My father had another year on that loan."

Lindsey dug her nails into her palms. It was an old habit, one she'd perfected before she'd been out of grade school as a way to keep Will from seeing how strongly he affected her. "Your father was dead. And you'd been gone a long time."

"I came back. And I would have turned the Claxton

Ranch around and made good on the loan. All I needed was a year."

"Who knew you'd stick around that long?"

Her statement struck home. She saw the guilt flicker across his features and instantly regretted her words. Fifteen years ago, he'd walked out on them all: his father, the ranch that had been in his family for three generations, and her.

"I'm sorry . . ." she started. "I didn't—"

Will raised his hand to cut her off and stepped back, the wall between them descending like the frigid Wyoming winter.

Then, as if to himself, he said, "Yeah, who knew?"

"Will, I—"

"Forget it."

She didn't want to forget it. She wanted to take back her words. Will might have deserted them all those years ago, but it wasn't like he'd gone off gallivanting around the world. He'd joined the Marines and served his country, and from what she'd heard through the small-town rumor mill, he'd served with distinction. Then, when he'd returned seven years ago, he'd more than proven himself. Despite losing his family's land, he'd stayed on in Willowbend, working as a ranch hand wherever he could. A few years back, he'd hired on as foreman of the Lazy W, one of the larger spreads in the area. It had been a gentleman's play-thing with an absentee owner until Will got hold of it and turned it into a highly profitable working ranch.

She wanted to tell him she was proud of him, of what he'd done both in the service and here at home, but his mood had changed. A moment ago, he'd been the macho cowboy she'd always known, pushing her, so sure of himself. Suddenly, he seemed older, less brash. The past had changed him, and she realized that she really didn't know him anymore.

Without another word, she turned and climbed into her truck. The last thing she saw as she pulled out of the parking lot of The Rusty Spur was Will Claxton's face: dark, forbidding, and more compelling than ever.

Will watched Lindsey drive away.

He would have liked nothing better than to climb into his own truck and head home, forgetting this night had ever happened. It seemed a fitting reaction to Lindsey's reality slap.

Jeremiah Baker hadn't stolen the Claxton Ranch, Will had lost it. He hadn't been here when his father needed him, and by the time Will had returned, it had been too late. His father was dead, and his family's heritage had become Baker property. As usual, Lindsey had gotten right to the heart of the matter.

If it didn't hurt so much, he could almost laugh.

He remembered Eric's comment that she'd hit a run of bad luck out on her ranch, the Silver Creek. For years, he'd avoided Lindsey and the rest of the Bakers: Jeremiah, while he lived, and Stuart. Still, Will had heard things.

He knew about Stuart's drinking and gambling and Lindsey's attempt to run the ranch by herself. Neither surprised Will. Lindsey had always been the stronger of the two Bakers, but he knew she couldn't do it alone. No one could. For years, Will had been planning and saving to repurchase the land he'd lost. He figured by the time he was ready to make Lindsey an offer, she'd be more than willing to sell off a piece of the ranch that had become too large for any one person to run alone. But this new bit of information, a string of accidents, bothered him, and he headed back into the Spur.

An hour later, he had more questions than answers. But one thing was clear—the Silver Creek was in serious trouble. For a moment, he considered returning home to the Lazy W and forgetting all about Lindsey and her problems.

He couldn't do it.

Despite everything that had come between them, she'd once been his best friend. Though he knew she'd never ask for help—especially from him—he planned to give it to her anyway. Besides, if she lost her ranch, she'd lose his land as well.

* * *

Morning came early to the Silver Creek Ranch.

Lindsey was out of bed a full hour before dawn, even though she'd gotten hardly any sleep. After she'd finally managed to get Stuart home the night before, she'd lain awake for hours, unable to rid her thoughts of a certain cowboy.

Damn Will Claxton.

She'd thought she'd outgrown her infatuation with him. After all, she was a grown woman, not the awkward girl who'd spent her childhood and half her adolescence traipsing after him. Not that Will had ever paid her any attention—at least not in the way she'd wanted. He'd had his pick of the prettiest girls around, and Lindsey . . . well, she'd been just one of the boys.

Then he'd gone away, and she didn't see him for eight years. She'd never quite forgiven him for that, for walking away from their friendship without so much as a backward glance. When he'd returned, the loss of his family's ranch had destroyed any chance they might have had to mend things between them. Since then, she'd occasionally seen him around; in a town the size of Willowbend, it couldn't be helped. They'd nod and say a brief hello, but Will had seemed as determined as she to avoid any further contact.

So why had he suddenly reappeared in her life?

He was a distraction she couldn't afford—even for one night. She had a ranch to run, a roundup to supervise, and far bigger problems than Will Claxton.

Over the past couple of months, the Silver Creek had been plagued with accidents. For a while, she'd believed it was just a string of bad luck. Now she knew better. After what she'd found yesterday, she couldn't ignore the reality that someone was deliberately trying to ruin her. But who? And why?

She thought of Will. Then immediately dismissed the idea.

He wanted his family's land—she knew that—but she couldn't believe he'd resort to bankrupting the Silver Creek to get it. They'd been friends and neighbors too long, their families' ranches prospering side by side for three generations. No, it couldn't be Will. She'd have to look somewhere else for the culprit.

But not now. Spring roundup started today, and she couldn't afford to think about anything else.

She found her foreman, Jim Horns, alone in the kitchen. Their cook had already headed down to help with the chuck wagon but had left hot biscuits in the oven, and ham and eggs on the stove. Lindsey filled her plate and joined Jim at the table.

"Have you seen Stuart this morning?" she asked.

"Not yet. I expect he'll be down soon."

Lindsey wasn't so sure. On the best of days, Stuart could be counted on to drag his feet. After last night, he was either hungover or still drunk. She wasn't sure which would be worse.

"If he isn't down by the time I'm finished eating," she said, "I'm going up after him."

"No need," Stuart said. "I'm here."

Lindsey turned toward her brother's voice. He looked shaky, standing at the bottom of the back stairs. Biting back her automatic impulse to chastise him, she said, "Come on and eat. You'll feel better."

Stuart made his way to the counter and poured himself a cup of coffee before settling heavily into the chair across from her. She started to suggest again that he eat but stopped herself. It would only make things worse between them. And actually, she sympathized with his lack of appetite; hers had vanished as well.

"We had another accident yesterday," she said instead.

Without responding, Stuart sipped at his coffee.

Lindsey tamped down her irritation at his lack of concern. "The fence was down in the high pasture."

"Fences break all the time."

"This one was cut. And someone drove a couple dozen head into the ravine."

He glanced at her briefly and then returned to his coffee. "Might have been Claxton."

She nearly dropped her cup, surprised and unnerved that Stuart had voiced her earlier thoughts.

"Seems to me he has a bone to pick," Stuart added.

"Maybe, but—" She stopped herself, realizing she'd been about to jump to Will's defense. And why? Because they'd once been friends? That had ended a long time ago, and she hardly knew the man now. She'd admitted as much last night. Besides, it was the first time Stuart had offered an opinion on their recent string of accidents. She couldn't dismiss it.

Just then she noticed Stuart's hands. He could barely hold his cup.

"Jim," she said. "Is there a good roper among the men?"

Stuart set down his cup and glared at her. Roping and branding were the top jobs of the day, given to the most senior hands. In the past, Stuart and Lindsey had roped. Jim had branded. The other jobs got divvied up between the regular hired hands and the temporary help brought in for the roundup.

"Well . . ." Jim glanced at Stuart before answering. "Al's an okay man with a rope."

"Good." Lindsey faced her brother. "Stuart, I want you to ride out and meet the herd coming in from the winter pasture. They're short a couple of men, and I want to make sure those cows make it in."

For a moment, he stared at her without saying a word, while she struggled with her decision. She'd just insulted him, and it wouldn't make their tenuous relationship any better.

"Why don't you just spit it out, Lindsey?" he said. "You want me out of the way."

She considered denying it, but what was the point? All three of them knew the truth. "Look at your hands. They're shaking. You're in no condition to rope today."

His eyes clouded with anger, and for a moment she thought he'd argue with her. Lord knew they'd had enough knock-down-drag-out fights in the six months since their father's death. Instead, Stuart pushed away from the table and stomped out of the kitchen, leaving a heavy silence behind him.

"Are you sure about this, Lindsey?" Jim asked.

"He can hardly walk."

"He'll sober up quick enough once he's in the saddle."

"And be hungover? I'm paying a half-dozen extra men by the hour. I can't afford to keep them any longer than necessary." She stood, her appetite gone. "With all the other problems around here, I can't risk the possibility that Stuart might mess up today."

Jim frowned, obviously disapproving of her methods. He'd been her father's foreman, hired away from the Claxton Ranch after it folded. Though he'd stayed on after her father's death, she'd always felt that Jim resented working for her.

She started toward the door, but stopped when he said, "Stuart might be right, you know."

Crossing her arms, she turned to face him. "About what?"

"About Claxton. He could have cut those fences."

"I don't believe it." Though the truth was, she didn't *want* to believe it.

"Why? Because you used to be sweet on him?"

She just barely reined in her anger. "We were friends. Nothing more."

"Don't matter." He shrugged in that superior old-timer way of his. "He's got more than enough reason to cause you trouble."

Jim and Stuart had a point. Will wanted the Claxton Ranch; he'd stated as much last night. She'd be a fool to ignore the possibility that he was behind their problems.

She was saved from further speculation when one of the younger cowboys appeared at the kitchen door. "Lindsey, you better come on out here. We got company."

She glanced at Jim, who shrugged. Then she headed outside with her foreman right behind her.

A dozen men, still on horseback, waited for her in the side yard. Right in front sat Will Claxton, disturbingly masculine on the back of a big Appaloosa stallion. "Morning, Lindsey."

She nodded. "Will." Then she forced herself to look around at the others before coming back to him. "You boys are out early."

He smiled. "It's branding day."

Crossing her arms, she met his smile with a raised eyebrow. "Then you should be back at the Lazy W."

"We thought maybe you could use a hand."

It was the last thing she expected. Though Lord knew she needed the help, especially with Stuart hungover and all the other problems that had left her shorthanded. But there was no way she'd admit any of that. "I'm sure you've got your own stock to tend."

Will settled deeper into his saddle. "That we do. But I thought it was about time we teamed up. Both our herds have gotten too big for one outfit to handle."

"Really?" It seemed a bit sudden. And too convenient. "Why now?"

"We're shorthanded."

She didn't buy it. Will's ranch, the Lazy W, was the biggest spread around, with a permanent crew large enough to handle roundup without hiring outside help. There was something else going on here. Was this part of Will's plan to get his hands on the Claxton Ranch? "This wouldn't by any chance have something to do with our conversation last night, would it?"

"We're just here to help."

She hesitated. "Why the sudden interest in the Silver Creek?"

Will gave her one of those half smiles of his. "There's nothing sudden about my interest in the Silver Creek."

"I suspect not." She moved closer, her anger stirring unexpectedly. Maybe she *was* being naive. Maybe Stuart and Jim were right. "And nothing would suit you better than for me to have to sell it. Or part of it, anyway."

He didn't deny it, and she didn't move or take her eyes off him. "No, thanks," she said finally. "We don't need your kind of help."

"Fine." Will leaned forward. "Let your cattle wander all over the range unbranded."

"They wouldn't wander if people didn't cut my fences."

He straightened in his saddle. "If you've got accusations to make, Lindsey, I suggest you take it up with the authorities."

She stepped back, putting distance between them. "I don't need your charity."

"If you aren't the most stubborn—"

Jim cut Will off. "Are you talking about a fair exchange of labor here, Claxton?"

Lindsey turned to her foreman, clamping down on her automatic reprimand. She didn't like him interfering, but she couldn't make an issue of it in front of the men.

Will kept his eyes on her. "You bet. I'll expect your entire crew at the Lazy W soon as we're done here."

Taking her arm, Jim pulled her aside. "It's not a bad offer, Lindsey."

"I don't believe you," she said, keeping her voice low. "A few minutes ago you were accusing him of cutting our fences. Now you want to work with him? Accept his help? It doesn't make any sense, Jim."

He shrugged. "If Claxton's here, we can keep an eye on him."

"And what about the roundup? I can't afford for anything to go wrong. If he's really behind our problems—"

"Our entire crew is here. And his. Plus, we'll be at the Lazy W in a day or two. He wouldn't dare try anything. Besides, we need the help."

Lindsey forced herself to calm down and think rationally. Jim was right. If Will was here, they could keep an eye on him. Besides, his offer made sense. The smaller ranches all worked together on roundup, pooling resources, shortening one of the most critical jobs of the year. Why not the larger ranches like the Lazy W and the Silver Creek?

Still, she hesitated, though there really wasn't much question that she'd accept his help. She might be stubborn, but she wasn't stupid. She was desperately shorthanded, and Will had offered a solution. Even though she suspected his motives, she'd be a fool to turn him down.

She walked back to where Will waited with his men. "Okay, you've got a deal." Only they were going to play by her rules. "We'll split the herd into two branding corrals and divide our men between them."

Smiling, Will climbed off his horse. "Sounds fine."

"And . . ." she added, "I need a good roper." The best way to keep an eye on Will was to watch him herself. She'd know if he was up to anything. "Do you have someone you can spare?"

"Will I do?"

She saw the amusement in his dark eyes and almost changed her mind. He'd known she couldn't turn his crew away, and she suspected he knew what she was trying to do now. But she wasn't about to back down.

"Fine," she said, keeping her voice neutral. "You'll be teaming up with me." Then, before he could say anything else, she added, "I have a few men bringing down the last of the herd from the winter pasture. They should be here in a couple of hours. Have your men help themselves to some coffee while we get geared up."

With that, she headed off to saddle her horse, putting distance between herself and Will Claxton. As she went, she called instructions to Jim. The butane brand heaters needed to be started and the irons heated; the rest of the crew were to mount up and cut the bulls from the herd and put them in separate pens.

She didn't notice Will following her into the barn until he grabbed her arm and spun her around to face him. "What the hell was that all about?" he demanded.

She stared pointedly at his hand and then raised her chin, meeting his angry stare. "You tell me." She pulled free of his grasp, barely resisting the urge to rub at the spot where he'd held her. "You're the one with the long-standing interest in the Silver Creek."

"You think I did it?"

Instead of answering, she headed into the tack room. Again, he followed her, and suddenly her decision to accept his offer seemed like a bad idea. Having Will around all day would have been difficult under the best circumstances. But she'd just made things worse by implying he was responsible for cutting her fences.

"You certainly have motive."

"You really think I'd resort to cutting your fences or damaging your equipment?" He planted his hands on his hips. "Or stealing your feed shipments for God's sake?"

Gathering her saddle and bridle, she said, "You seem to know a lot about it."

"Everyone knows."

She stopped abruptly and stared at him.

"Every cowhand in the whole damn county knows about your problems, Lindsey."

Her stomach tightened, but she fought to keep her expression neutral. He stood blocking her exit from the tack room, his face unreadable. Even his eyes, his wonderfully expressive eyes, seemed unfathomable.

"After you left the Spur last night," he said, "I got curious about what was going on out here. So I asked around."

"If you wanted information about the Silver Creek, you should have come to me."

"Funny thing about that, Lindsey. Somehow I didn't think you'd be too forthcoming with the information."

There was no way to answer that. He was right, of course. She'd have told him, or anyone else who asked, to mind his own business. But it seemed it was too late for that. News of her "accidents" had gotten out. Suddenly, she realized that whoever was trying to ruin her might just succeed. Rumors were insidious things. They had a way of making things happen.

"If you'll get out of my way," she said, "I've got to get saddled up."

He stepped aside, allowing her to make her escape, but he wasn't done with her. He followed her to the horse's stall. "I won't lie to you, Lindsey. I want the Claxton Ranch back."

She kept her eyes on her work, on the smooth leather of her saddle and the strong, reliable back of her mare.

"But what's happening here isn't my style," he said. "You of all people should know that."

She tightened the cinch on her saddle, still refusing to look at him. "Just what is your style?" She heard the strain in her voice and hoped Will hadn't noticed.

"I want to buy it from you, fair and square."

"And if I won't sell?"

"Everyone has a price, Lindsey."

She looked at him then, unable to stop herself. "Not everyone," she said coldly.

"That's where you're wrong." Tipping his hat to her, he turned and headed back outside.

She waited until he was out of sight before closing her eyes and resting her forehead against the sleek neck of her mare. She wanted desperately to believe that Will had nothing to do with the accidents plaguing her ranch, but she couldn't kid herself. She recognized a warning when she heard one. Will wanted the Claxton Ranch and planned to go after it.

Unfortunately, she couldn't sell, even if she wanted to. She'd made a promise, and promises were meant to be kept.

* * *

As always, work eased Will's mood.

After his strained encounter with Lindsey, he needed it badly. It infuriated him that she actually thought he'd resort to vandalism and theft to regain control of his family's land. He wasn't a criminal. Besides, as angry as he'd been with her these past seven years, he would never intentionally hurt her. She of all people should know that.

As for working with her, he had to admit they made a good team. But then, they'd grown up together. At one time or another, they'd shared about every ranch chore imaginable. It only took a short while for the years to slip away, and they were just Lindsey and Will again, best friends, taking pleasure in trying to outdo each other.

Yet there was a difference, one Will became more

painfully aware of with each passing minute. Lindsey was no longer a little girl, a tomboy out to show up the boys. She'd become a woman. It was obvious in every move: the way her thighs gripped the saddle as she eased into the herd and singled out a calf, the pull and tug of her shirt as she swung the rope, the purely feminine smile of triumph when she snagged the animal's hind legs. He wondered why none of the other cowboys had noticed, why one of them hadn't snagged *her*.

His preoccupation with Lindsey was probably why he didn't spot the lone horseman barreling into the yard until the newcomer's horse, nostrils flaring and sides heaving, pranced near the gate.

Lindsey pulled in her rope and headed for the fence. "Jack, what is it?"

"There was an accident. The herd . . ." The boy paused to catch his breath.

"What about the herd?" Her voice rose in apprehension. "What happened?"

"A rockslide. Just as they started through the pass."

Chapter Three

Will slid to the ground and grabbed the boy's bridle, calming his horse with a few soothing words. "Settle down, son. And tell us what's going on."

The boy nodded, visibly taking a deep breathe. "We set off at first light, driving the herd in from the winter pasture." He glanced briefly at Lindsey, but continued talking to Will. "We'd just reached the pass at the north end when I heard an explosion. Next thing I knew, it was like the whole mountain was coming down on top of us."

The color drained from Lindsey's face. "Was anybody hurt?"

He shook his head. "No ma'am. We were lucky. Another few minutes, and we'd have been trapped. As it was, we got out with a few cuts and bruises."

"And the herd?"

"We lost a few. Maybe a half dozen. But the pass is blocked. Stuart tried to call, but you how spotty reception is up there. So, he sent me. I had to come over the south ridge."

Lindsey closed her eyes briefly, obviously shaken.

Will's first impulse was to wrap an arm around her, but he stopped himself. Lindsey wouldn't appreciate it in front of her men—especially after accusing him of causing her problems. So he kept his hands to himself and shifted his attention to the young cowboy.

"Okay, Jack . . ." he started. "That's your name, right?"

"Yes, sir."

"Come on down. You did good getting here this quick."

The boy climbed off his horse, and by that time, Lindsey had regained her composure. "Jack, I want you to call Sheriff Farley," she said. "Use the house phone and tell him everything you just told us."

"Are you going out there?"

"This has gone on long enough," she said firmly. "Have the sheriff meet me. Better yet, wait for him here, and then bring him out yourself. You'll have to come around through the south end of the valley."

Jack nodded. "Okay."

"I'm coming with you, Lindsey," Will said.

Her gaze snapped to his. "This is my responsibility. Not yours."

He wasn't about to argue with her. It wouldn't do any good. He'd never convince her, but he planned on going whether she wanted him along or not. "I'm going."

She opened her mouth to reply just as Jim stepped forward. "You go on, Lindsey. And take Will with you." She turned her angry eyes on her foreman, but he kept on talking. "You shouldn't be going out there alone. I'll keep the crews working and make sure Jack and the sheriff connect when he arrives."

It was the second time today Jim had stepped in and countered her. From the look on her face, Will knew she didn't like it. Right now, though, he appreciated the support.

"Look at it this way, Lindsey," he said, trying to soften the blow. "You'll be able to keep an eye on me."

She stood her ground a moment longer, looking back and forth between the two men. Then she nodded and glanced briefly at Will before directing Jim. "No matter what happens, I want this crew over at the Lazy W as soon as you're done with the roundup here."

"I'll see to it," Jim agreed.

Within minutes, Jack was inside calling the sheriff, and Lindsey and Will set off on horseback.

It was a good hour's ride, and Will kept his silence the whole way. He didn't like what was happening here, and he sure as hell didn't like being accused of causing it. Problems on the Silver Creek meant trouble for him as well. Lindsey, owning and operating a ranch grown too large, was his best shot at once again gaining control of his family's land. But what really concerned him was Lindsey.

He watched her closely as they rode. She tried to hide it, but the strain of this last accident showed. She sat a little straighter in her saddle, one hand clenched on her thigh, her nails digging into her palms, while her mare fidgeted beneath her.

He knew what she must be thinking, because he'd had the same thoughts himself. Someone who would start a rock slide above a mountain pass, with men and cattle below, was capable of anything. Even murder.

It was well past noon when they arrived at the pass. Jack hadn't exaggerated. It was completely blocked by man-size boulders and a variety of smaller rocks. It would take a dynamite crew a couple of days to clear it.

Will's first inclination was to climb to the top of the

cliff. Jack had said he'd heard an explosion before the avalanche, and Will wanted to have a look around. Lindsey, on the other hand, wanted to get to her men as quickly as possible.

It took them another hour to ride the long way around, over a ridge that was only passable on horseback. Finally, they rode down into the Silver Creek's winter pasture, a long sweet meadow nestled between hills of ponderosa pine. A spring-fed stream traveled its length, with fresh grass and clusters of purple and white crocus covering the valley floor. At one time, it had been the northern boundary of the Claxton Ranch and one of Will's favorite spots.

Shoving the memory aside, he followed Lindsey into the meadow. They quickly located the herd. It had been moved to the far end of the field, away from the pass.

Stuart rode out to meet them. He glanced briefly at Will but spoke to his sister. "I arrived right after it happened."

"Is everyone all right?" she asked. Though Jack had already assured her the men were okay, Will understood Lindsey's need to verify it.

"Nothing serious," Stuart answered. "We lost a wagon and some cattle."

"How many?"

While Stuart recounted the damages, Will listened with half an ear, his eyes scanning the cliffs on either side of the pass. He wanted to get up there and look around. If they waited until the sheriff arrived, it could be too late. A sudden storm or high wind would destroy any existing evidence.

"Lindsey, go check on your men," he said. "I'm climbing up there to see what I can find."

Stuart frowned. "What concern is it of yours?"

"He came to help," Lindsey said, surprising Will that

31

she'd take his side against her brother. Then to Will, she added, "I'm coming with you."

"No need. See to your crew."

"It's *my* ranch, Will."

He met her gaze for a moment and saw her suspicions. She might have defended him to her brother, but she was a long way from trusting him. "You're right," he answered, ignoring the sting of her doubt. "It's your ranch. Let's go."

"I'll come too," Stuart offered.

"No." Lindsey pulled away from her brother. "You stay with the herd. We'll be back in an hour or so."

Stu's eyes flashed angrily, and Will wondered if he shared his sister's suspicions, or if he just didn't like taking orders from her. But at the moment, Stuart was the least of Will's concerns. Somebody was getting very serious about stirring up trouble on the Silver Creek. If they weren't stopped, someone could get hurt.

Leaving Stuart behind, Will and Lindsey started up the hill on the north side of the pass. They rode as far as they could, then hobbled their horses and continued on foot. It was an easy climb, and within a half hour, they'd reached the top.

"What are we looking for?" Lindsey asked.

"I'm not sure. Anything that indicates someone was up here this morning. You take this side, I'll check—"

"We're staying together," she cut in.

His temper snapped. "Dammit, Lindsey, I didn't ambush your herd. I was at your place this morning. Remember?"

She stared at him defiantly. "You could have set the blast before showing up."

He mumbled a curse, his hands on his waist.

"That would have been some trick. We're an hour's ride

from the Silver Creek and an hour and a half from the Lazy W. Your man started back right after the blast, about the same time my crew and I showed up in your yard. Just how do you think I managed to be in both places at the same time?"

"I don't know. Maybe you used a timer of some kind."

"And I knew exactly when your herd would be heading through this pass?"

She hesitated, turning away from him to stare off into the distance.

"Come on, Lindsey," he prodded. "You know me. You know I couldn't—"

"That's just it, Will." She brought her gaze back to meet his. "I don't know you at all. Not anymore."

Her statement stung. Though in truth, he couldn't argue with her. She was right. A lot of time and bad feelings had passed between them in the past seven years. But right now, none of that mattered. She was in trouble, and he needed to convince her that he wasn't the enemy, that they both had something at stake here.

"Look, we both know you were lucky today," he said, changing tactics. "The next time this guy pulls something, someone could end up dead." She flinched, but he pushed on. "You have to trust me, Lindsey."

"Why? Why should I trust you?"

"Because . . ." He paused, searching for the words to convince her. "You need me. At least for now."

He watched the play of emotions on her features and realized she was frightened—though only someone who knew her well would see it. He couldn't blame her. This last incident had raised the stakes.

"All right, Will," she said finally. "I'm willing to admit that you probably didn't have anything to do with this rock slide. And, at the moment, I could use the help. But trust . . ." Her voice trailed off and she shook her head. "Trust has to be earned."

He sighed and looked away, then nodded and said, "Okay. I guess I can't ask for more than that."

"No," she said. "You can't." With that, she walked off.

He almost went after her, but as much as he wanted to settle this between them, now wasn't the time. He needed to keep his priorities straight. The land, and finding out who was responsible for Lindsey's troubles, was what he should be concentrating on. There would be time later for them to hash out their differences.

Moving in the opposite direction as she, he started searching the ground for clues. A few minutes later, Lindsey called to him.

"Will, over here." She'd squatted down next to some bushes, her eyes focused on the ground. "Look at this."

He came up behind her. "Well, well, someone was careless." Leaning over, he picked up a bit of wick-like rope. "Trimming a fuse and leaving pieces of it behind." He shook his head and slipped the evidence into his shirt pocket. "Doesn't seem too bright, does it?" Taking her arm, he pulled Lindsey to her feet. "Made any enemies lately, Linds?"

Bewilderment shadowed her face. "Not that I know of."

"What about our friend Gus?"

"I guess it's possible." She shrugged. "But I didn't even know he existed until last night, and these accidents have been going on for a couple of months."

"I found out last night that he and his pal have been hanging around town for weeks. Maybe longer," Will told her. "And this may not be connected to the other incidents.

It's certainly a step beyond cut fences and delayed feed shipments."

She thought about it for a moment, and then shook her head. "It doesn't make sense. There just wasn't enough time for Gus to plan something like this. First off, how could he have known we'd be bringing a herd through this particular pass today? He would have had . . . what? About five hours to get that information and set it all up? I don't think so." She paused, letting her gaze wander along the edge of the cliff and down toward the blocked pass. "Besides, I can't believe the accidents aren't connected. It would just be too much of a coincidence."

Will agreed, but he'd wanted to hear her say it.

Someone was trying to force her out, to make her lose the Silver Creek. The rock slide had just been a more direct attack than the previous accidents. The question was why. Was it vengeance or an attempt to force her to sell her land? If he could answer that question, he might have a clue as to who was responsible.

By unspoken agreement, neither of them mentioned the fuse when they got back down the hill.

Lindsey sent Stuart and half the crew back to the ranch to help with the roundup and branding. Stuart protested, especially when Will announced he was staying, but again, Lindsey overrode his objections. Along with the men left behind, Will and Lindsey spent the rest of the day rounding up strays and watching for any further signs of trouble.

Late in the afternoon, Jim showed up with a pickup full of fresh supplies and bad news. Sheriff Farley couldn't make it out until the next morning. Lindsey decided to remain with the herd and didn't argue when Will said he would stay as well. They'd start back tomorrow, going the long way around the hills, once the sheriff showed up and had time to look around.

After Jim left, Lindsey rode off alone to the far side of the herd. Will let her go and eventually lost sight of her. The past twenty-four hours had been rough on her, and knowing Lindsey, she needed some time alone. As the sun sank toward the western horizon, he sent the crew into camp for dinner. Come sundown and throughout the night, they'd work in shifts.

But first, he and Lindsey needed to talk.

He knew where he'd find her, sitting on a shelf of rock that jutted out from the cliff face on the east side of the valley. When they'd still been in grade school, they'd discovered a series of handholds and footholds that enabled them to reach the ledge. It had become their secret spot, a place to run whenever they'd wanted to hide from the adult world.

She glanced at him briefly as he climbed up next to her.

For several minutes, neither of them spoke as the setting sun painted the sky with vivid streaks of red and pink. The spectacle nearly took his breath away. He'd spent eight years away from these mountains, and never found anything to compare with their beauty.

"I haven't been up here in years," he said. Not since he'd returned to Willowbend and found this land belonged to Jeremiah Baker.

"Running a ranch doesn't leave much time for watching sunsets."

"No," he agreed. "It doesn't."

An awkward silence stretched between them. It shouldn't be this way. He couldn't count the number of hours they'd spent in this exact spot when they were kids.

They'd been as close as any brother and sister, closer actually than Lindsey had ever been to Stuart. But so much time had passed. Too many things had changed. Hell, *they'd* changed.

"Lindsey, what you said earlier—about not knowing me anymore—" For years, he'd avoided this topic. Regret and guilt had kept him silent. "I never meant for things to turn out this way between us."

She looked at him and frowned. "What did you expect?" There was no accusation in her voice, only sadness. "After what happened."

He thought back to the day Jeremiah Baker had taken possession of the Claxton Ranch. Will had wanted Lindsey to intervene, and they'd argued bitterly, both saying things they hadn't meant, hurtful words they couldn't easily retract. "I was so angry."

"You asked me to take sides, to choose between you and my father."

"I know how close the two of you were." Lindsey's mother had died when Stuart was still a toddler, and Jeremiah Baker had raised his two children alone. Lindsey had adored her father.

"He was always there for me. While you . . ." She shrugged and looked away. "You left without even saying good-bye. And for eight years, no one heard a word from you. Then you showed back up and expected—"

"I expected you to trust me."

She looked at him and nodded. "Yeah."

"Like now."

Again, she nodded and looked away.

"I was wrong. And . . ." Though he knew the words wouldn't make up for the past, he had to say them. "I'm sorry."

Silence, once again.

Finally, Lindsey spoke. "Remember the night we camped up here?"

Surprised at the sudden shift of topics, he let out a short laugh. "How could I forget? Dad nearly took my hide off for that one. He thought I'd taken advantage of you or something." He'd been sixteen and Lindsey thirteen. Until that night, it had never occurred to him that anyone would misinterpret their relationship. He'd never even thought of her in that way. To him, Lindsey had been just . . . well . . . Lindsey.

"If only he'd known," she said, breaking into his thoughts. "You spent the entire night moaning about what's-her-name."

"Oh, yeah." He grinned, remembering. "Amy Lou Bentley. She broke my heart." He laughed again. "But I *never* moaned."

"Hah!"

"What about you?" He glanced at her, wondering why she'd chosen this particular direction for their conversation. "Seems to me I spent enough time listening to you. You were always bellyaching about some boy who thought he could outride or out rope you."

She smiled smugly and said, "None of them ever could."

"No." He had to laugh. "They couldn't."

Again, the silence stretched between them, a little easier this time. More like the two old friends than the adversaries they'd become. Maybe that's what she'd intended, taking them back to the good memories, while they examined the bad.

Pulling off her hat, she settled back against the rock.

Will realized he liked looking at her and being able to

see her face, with its smooth, pale skin framed by her fiery hair. He wondered if she still hated her hair color as she had when they were kids. Back then, he hadn't understood what the big deal was. Who cared what color her hair was?

What a fool he'd been. Her hair was beautiful, like fire from the setting sun.

"You know . . ." Again, she broke the silence and into his thoughts. "Before you left, I never believed you'd really go."

That surprised him. Of all people, he'd thought she understood.

"Oh, I know you'd been talking about joining the marines for over a year," she explained. "I guess I just never thought you'd really do it."

"You know how it was between Dad and me. We were always fighting about something." Usually the ranch. "We couldn't seem to agree on anything. I had to get away."

"I know. I guess I just . . ." She shrugged, not bothering to finish her sentence. Then, after a moment, she said quietly, "You should have said good-bye."

Regret wrapped itself around him like an old familiar coat. There were so many things he would change if he could. This was only one of them. Pulling off his hat, he dropped it on the ground and ran a hand through his hair.

"Dad and I had one hell of a fight the day I left. Funny . . ." He laughed briefly and without humor. "I don't even remember *what* we fought about." He turned to look at her. "But I had it in my head that I had to leave that night or I'd never get away." He hesitated, and then added, "But you're right. I should have said good-bye."

After a moment, she nodded and turned away. "It doesn't matter now."

He laid a hand on her arm. "I missed you."

"Me too." She looked at him, smiling tentatively, and

the freshness of it washed over him like a new day. It enveloped him like spring sunshine after a long cold winter, warming him to the core.

"You should smile more often," he said.

His words shattered the moment. Her smile flickered and died, and wariness crept into her eyes. He realized suddenly that he'd frightened her, and it amazed him. He didn't like the idea of Lindsey being afraid. Especially of him.

"Don't . . ." he started, capturing a stray curl between his fingertips. He'd meant only to reassure her that she had nothing to fear from him. Instead, his hand seemed to move of its own volition to free her thick, strawberry-blond hair from the band holding it away from her face. He wanted to see it fanned out about her shoulders, catching the last rays of the setting sun.

Her eyes widened at his touch, bright green, the color of spring grass, new and shiny with the promise of summer in their depths. He wanted to kiss her.

The realization jarred him, and he dropped his hand. "I'm sorry."

She reached up and touched her hair briefly, then quickly turned away. He watched her face, aware of the confusion playing across her features. He understood how she felt. He'd known this woman all his life, and yet, he felt like he was seeing her for the first time.

After a few minutes, she said, "Will, what I said last night . . ." She hesitated. "About you not sticking around long enough to save the Claxton Ranch."

"It doesn't matter, Lindsey."

"I didn't mean it."

Will sighed. "You *were* right, you know. How could your father or anyone else know what I would do? I'd been gone eight years." He paused. "Hell, I'm not sure I knew myself."

"I knew," she said simply. "I told my father he was wrong."

Lindsey felt his gaze on her but kept hers focused straight ahead. She couldn't turn to him, couldn't look into his dark eyes without losing herself. All her old feelings for him had risen up to taunt her, without the old defenses she'd once kept so firmly in place. She was too aware of him sitting next to her, his broad shoulders brushing hers, his long legs stretched out beside her.

"Lindsey?" There was a question in his voice. A question she dared not answer. Then he touched her, a gentle finger under her chin, turning her face to his once again. She didn't resist. Couldn't.

"Thank you," he said.

"For what?" She could barely get the words past the lump in her throat.

"For understanding. For believing in me."

He should have released her then. He should have removed his hand and let her turn away. He didn't. Instead, he toyed with her hair again, and for a moment, she couldn't breathe. Then his hand found its way to the back of her neck, and tension coiled like a viper in her stomach.

He was going to kiss her.

She knew it as surely as she knew his name. It was what she wanted. What she'd dreamed about her entire life. Yet it frightened her beyond words. Still, she couldn't have stopped him if her life depended on it. Because right now, she needed to feel his lips on hers more than she needed her next breath.

Chapter Four

Magic. Will's mouth was magic.

He brushed his lips against hers gently, coaxing her mouth open. He slowly deepened the kiss, his tongue seeking hers while he urged her closer with the lightest pressure of his fingers on her neck.

With a soft sigh, Lindsey sank against him.

She'd fantasized about this a million times—kissing Will, touching him. It had been the recurring theme of her adolescent daydreams. But nothing she'd ever imagined came close to the reality of his lips on hers. He was gentle and demanding all at once, seducing her with his mouth, making her ache for more than just this simple touch.

She thought of all the years they'd wasted, the time they'd spent apart when this potent sensation lay within their reach. Why had they waited so long? Why . . .

Reality swept through her like a January snowstorm.

There was no *they*. Each of them had wanted something different. She'd always wanted Will, but he hadn't been interested. He'd never kissed her before because he hadn't thought of her as a woman. She'd been his best friend, just one of the guys.

She pulled abruptly away from him and scrambled to her feet. "What the hell do you think you're doing?" she demanded.

He smiled, that slow, sexy smile she'd seen him use on other women. "I'd think that was obvious."

His teasing sparked her anger. "Oh, it's obvious all right." She crossed her arms, trapping her trembling hands. "I can't believe you'd sink so low."

He looked genuinely surprised, and he stood, taking a step toward her. "What are you talking about?"

"Stay where you are." She held up a hand to warn him off. "I don't want you to touch me."

"Look, whatever's wrong—"

She didn't let him finish. "Don't try to con me, Will Claxton." She'd regained a bit of her composure and with it the determination to call him on his game. "I've known you too long."

"Come on, Lindsey." With a sigh, he ran a hand through his hair. "It was only a kiss."

"Only a kiss!" She heard the note of hysteria in her voice and realized she wasn't as composed as she'd thought.

Dropping his hands to his hips, Will looked frustrated, then apologetic. "Look, I'm sorry. I didn't mean to upset you."

"Why did you kiss me?"

The question seemed to take him aback, and for a moment, he didn't answer. Finally, he shook his head and said, "I don't know. It just seemed like the thing to do."

"Just like that? After all these years?"

"Yeah. Just like that." Anger flared in his eyes, but Lindsey was too angry herself to care.

"I don't suppose kissing me has anything to do with the Claxton Ranch?"

He shook his head in disbelief. "God, Lindsey, you can't think—"

"You thought you'd try your legendary charm on me. Soften me up a bit so I'd reconsider your offer to buy that land," she said flatly.

"No."

"I can just imagine what they're saying about me in town. 'Poor little Lindsey, all alone now that her father's gone. Except for her brother Stuart.'" She let out a short, bitter laugh. "'And everyone knows he's no help. She needs a man to take care of her.'"

"You're about the least helpless woman I know, Lindsey." He took a step toward her, his expression tight. "And I've never said or thought otherwise."

"Exactly." She met his gaze head-on. "So why now, Claxton? Unless you thought you could seduce me into selling out."

His dark eyes flashed. "You can't believe that."

"Can't I? From where I stand, I'd be a fool not to." Sidestepping him, she grabbed her hat from the ground where she'd dropped it. "You know, Will, I'd almost rather you were the one sabotaging my operation. Somehow, that would seem more honest than what you just tried."

"This is crazy—"

"I want you gone first thing in the morning. Take your men and head on back to the Lazy W. I don't need your kind of help."

"Lindsey—"

"I mean it. I can't have men around me who I don't trust. And obviously, you fit that description." She started for the rim of the ledge, then turned back to him. "You know, you're right. These accidents aren't your style. You're more likely to seduce your victims."

* * *

Will watched Lindsey walk away, her accusations echoing in his head. His first impulse was to go after her, to make her come back and hash this out. Instead, settling back on the cold rock, he replayed the scene over and over in his mind.

What the hell had happened?

Despite what she thought, he hadn't climbed up on this ledge to seduce her. He'd wanted to talk to her and settle a few things between them, not create more problems. Kissing her had just seemed like the thing to do at the moment.

Kissing Lindsey.

He let out a short laugh and shook his head. It had just about knocked him flat. Who would have guessed she'd have such a sweet, responsive mouth? For a moment, he'd forgotten everything but the feel of her lips under his. Their shared past, their uncertain future, the land that stood between them; it had all vanished before the pleasure of something as simple as a kiss.

The whole thing was crazy.

He'd known Lindsey all their lives, but before last night when she'd stormed into the Spur, he'd never really thought of her sexually. That much of her accusation *was* true. But one touch of her lips and he'd never be able to think of her as just a friend again. Only, it looked like she wasn't about to let him anywhere near her. She'd pulled away from him, madder than a cornered she-wolf.

He'd sensed her vulnerability the moment he'd touched her, and knew that they were treading on shaky ground. There was always an initial shyness and uncertainty in a new relationship, but they were taking an old relationship and redefining it. Somehow, that was even more frightening.

He'd wanted to draw her further into his arms and reassure her, but when she'd accused him of using her to regain control of the Claxton Ranch, he'd hesitated. Because, in all honesty, he wasn't sure himself that she was safe from him.

For seven years, he'd worked tirelessly to reclaim his family's land, and Lindsey stood between him and that goal. She'd accused him of kissing her because of what he wanted from her.

He couldn't say for sure she was wrong.

Hours later, as he rode the outskirts of the herd, he watched a spring storm approach. For most of the night, the sky had been clear and bright with a million stars stretched across an obsidian sky. Then the wind had picked up and the distant lights had blinked out one by one. Pulling out his slicker, he slipped it on just as the heavens opened and released their burden.

He'd drawn the late watch, which was fine with him. He doubted whether he could sleep anyway—not with thoughts of Lindsey still rattling around in his head. Might as well let some other cowboy get a few extra hours of shut-eye. But as the deluge plastered the rain gear against his skin, his musings took a different bent. He thought of the evidence he and Lindsey might have missed up on the ridge: footprints or other clues to the identity of the person who'd started the rock slide. The storm would wash everything clean.

Too bad it couldn't do the same for him.

* * *

When Lindsey awoke the next morning Will was gone.

According to one of her men, he'd left before sunrise, heading back to the Lazy W. Her disappointment surprised her. She'd told him to leave, and she'd meant it. She had a ranch to save, and Will Claxton was an added complication she didn't need. He'd already cost her two nights' rest when she could least afford it.

Exhausted as she'd been last night, not even the storm had helped her sleep. Any other time, the steady downpour would have soothed her, lulling her into a deep sleep. Instead, thoughts of Will had occupied her. She'd tried to hold on to her certainty that his only interest was the Claxton land claimed by her father. But it was Will's kiss she remembered. His kiss that had left her restless and uneasy, aching for something she shouldn't want. And angry at herself for wanting it anyway.

Now he was gone. She should feel relieved. But even as she got her men started and the herd moving, her thoughts slipped back to Will. She found herself watching for him, wondering why he'd chosen this particular time to heed her wishes. Lord knew he'd ignored them often enough before.

The sheriff showed up about midmorning.

Lindsey and her crew had reached the south end of the valley and were moving across the low ridge separating them from the main part of her ranch. Leaving the herd with one of her senior hands, she went with the sheriff back to the pass. As she'd expected, there was nothing left to find —if there had been anything else there to begin with. The wind and rain the night before had swept the cliff clean.

The sheriff had asked a few questions—pretty much the

same questions she and Will had asked yesterday, and told her he'd look into it. At this point, there wasn't anything else he could do. Then he'd driven her back to the herd.

His last words to her had been a warning.

"Be careful, Lindsey," he'd said, and his words echoed through her for the rest of the afternoon. It wasn't what he'd said that bothered her, but what he hadn't said. Anyone who'd risk killing a dozen men by starting a rock slide was dangerous. If Lindsey and her ranch were his targets, there was no telling what he might try next.

After the sheriff left, she stayed with the herd until they set up camp a couple of miles out from the main buildings of the Silver Creek. Then she rode the rest of the way alone, reaching the ranch by late afternoon.

The yard was empty. Dismounting, she unsaddled her horse and turned her loose in the corral. There were still several hours of daylight left and probably a dozen chores needing her attention, but they'd have to wait. The strain of the past twenty-four hours weighed on her. She needed to regroup. An early dinner and hot bath, followed by a full eight hours of sleep sounded like heaven. In the morning, things would be clearer and she'd figure out what to do next.

She started toward the barn to store her gear. As she neared the back of the structure, she heard voices coming from the tack room.

"This is what happens when a woman don't know her place," said her foreman, Jim Horns. "Things get crazy."

"I don't know, Jim." Lindsey couldn't place the second voice. "She seems okay to me."

"How the hell would you know, boy? You're still wet behind the ears yourself."

The boy mumbled something Lindsey couldn't hear.

"You think any of this would have happened if Jeremiah

Baker were still alive? Think he would have tolerated someone cutting his fences or damaging his equipment? Hell no. Most likely, it's some jealous ex-boyfriend. Or even Will Claxton. That boy's got a mighty big bone to pick. Of course, he ain't the only one."

Lindsey had heard enough. It was bad enough that some unknown enemy was out to ruin her, she couldn't also have dissension among her men. Especially from her foreman, the man she depended on the most.

She stepped into the room. "So who else has a bone to pick with me, Jim? You?"

Both men turned. The boy, a temporary hand she'd hired for the roundup, flushed crimson. Jim, on the other hand, looked her right in the eye. It occurred to her he might have had something to do with all the accidents happening around the place. Then she dismissed the idea. What would he have to gain?

"I better be going," said the young hand, tipping his hat to Lindsey and sliding past her out the door.

Silence followed his exit.

She wasn't about to speak. It was up to Jim to explain himself. If he could.

Finally, he said, "So, you heard."

"Yes. I heard."

"Maybe it's just as well."

She crossed her arms, looking at the man who'd been her father's foreman for ten years, and braced herself against his betrayal. "I'm sorry you feel that way."

"I ain't staying, Lindsey."

For a moment, she couldn't respond.

"Got me another job offer," he said before she could ask. "Afraid it was just too good to pass up."

"I didn't know you were looking."

His gaze fell to his boots. "Things just aren't the same as they used to be around here. Since . . ." He looked straight at her then. "Well, since your pa passed away."

"And now you're working for a woman." She couldn't stop the sarcasm, and at this point, she wasn't sure she wanted to.

"Things might be different if Stuart—"

"If Stuart what? Was in charge?" She laughed abruptly. "Yeah, we'd probably be bankrupt by now instead of just heading in that direction."

He looked embarrassed again. "I'll stay the week and finish the roundup."

"No need." Anger washed through her. "Gather your things and come on up to the house. I'll pay you, and you can be on your way." Turning away before she said something she'd regret, she started for the door.

"Lindsey . . ."

She heard the guilt in his voice and steeled herself against it. Stopping, she kept her back to him. "I'll have a check ready in fifteen minutes." Then she left, walking fast, trying to outwalk the tears.

She wouldn't cry. She'd be damned before she let any of them see her cry.

Outside, she'd barely registered the early evening air before running smack into Will. "What the hell are you doing back here?" she snapped. Though she'd never been happier to see anyone in her life.

Grabbing her arms as if to steady her, he said, "I just had a talk with one of your men. He told me Jim Horns has taken another job. It looks like you need me after all."

Chapter Five

W ill smiled as Lindsey pushed him away.

"Like hell," she said, looking like an avenging angel with wisps of fire-bright hair framing her face and anger in her green eyes. "You're the last person I need." She stepped around him and headed for the house.

This was the Lindsey who Will knew and loved: the fighter. And after what he'd just overheard, she'd need every bit of courage she possessed.

He'd never much cared for Jim Horns, even though he knew the man was generally reliable and a competent fore-man. Just something about him had always bothered Will. He'd figured it had to do with the years Horns had worked for Will's father. Will had been an arrogant kid, and Horns hadn't had much tolerance for his boss's son. His leaving Lindsey in the lurch, however, made Will think there might be more substance to his dislike for the other man than Will's adolescent resentment.

Taking his time, he followed Lindsey to the house, not

bothering to knock before going inside. He found her behind her father's desk, a checkbook open in front of her.

"I thought I told you I didn't want you around," she said without looking up from her furious scribbling.

"You said you wanted me gone by this morning. And I was."

She looked up at him and scowled. "That's not funny, Will. You know what I meant."

"Yeah." He lowered himself into one of the worn chairs across from her desk. "I do. And I seriously considered it. Got all the way back to the Lazy W in fact."

"So why are you here?"

"I just couldn't do it, Linds."

She rolled her eyes. "Do what?"

"I couldn't leave you on your own."

She suddenly seemed at a loss for words—a miracle where Lindsey was concerned. Abruptly, she returned to filling out the draft. Just as she tore it from the checkbook with an angry rip, Jim Horns entered the room.

He glanced at Will and frowned. "What's he doing here?"

Lindsey leaned back in her chair, mimicking a posture Will had seen her father use a hundred times, a posture that was a not-so-subtle reminder of who was boss. Will could only guess at the effort it cost her under the circumstances.

"I believe you've just given up the right to ask me that question," she said. "Or any other question for that matter."

For a moment, Horns looked like he might shuffle his feet, like a recalcitrant schoolboy. Then he regained some of his earlier bravado. "Ten years working for your pa gives me the right. And the obligation." He motioned toward Will. "This is the kind of thing I was talking about. You ain't got no sense, Lindsey. Bringing—"

Will stood and faced the other man. "I think that's about enough, Horns."

"Will," Lindsey snapped.

He looked at her and saw the warning in her eyes. This was her battle, and she wanted him to let her fight it. Will eased back, and she switched her attention to Horns.

"Here's what I owe you." She stood and extended the check.

"Lindsey . . ." Jim stepped forward and took the payment. "Damn it. It shouldn't end like this."

"No, it shouldn't." She closed the checkbook with a resonating thud and stared at him, her face void of expression. "Good-bye, Jim."

After a moment, he looked away and, after a quick glance at Will, left the room.

Neither Will nor Lindsey spoke until the sound of the front door slamming echoed through the house. Then Lindsey sank back into her chair, her cheeks flushed.

"Well, that was fun." Sarcasm dripped from her voice.

Will chuckled. Leave it to Lindsey to get a rush out of an old-fashioned face-off. "Never did care much for ol' Jim."

"Me neither." She laughed shortly. "But he worked for my father for a long time."

"And mine," Will reminded her.

She gave him a half smile. "Yeah, and yours." For a moment, a compatible silence settled around them. Finally, Lindsey said, "Okay. Now, where were we?"

"I think you were getting ready to kick me off your ranch again." He settled back, letting her know he wasn't going anywhere.

"Oh, yeah. I was, wasn't I?"

"Look, Lindsey, I know you're determined to handle this situation by yourself . . ."

"This situation?" She arched an eyebrow.

"You know," he matched the sarcasm in her voice. "Someone cutting your fences and deliberately starting rock slides. That kind of thing."

"Oh, that."

"Yeah, that. You need help."

When she didn't respond right away, Will's thoughts slipped back to the previous evening on the ledge. She'd claimed he was untrustworthy, and the accusation had stuck with him ever since. Once again, he had to ask himself: Could she trust him? Looking at her, at the tension lining her pale face, he knew the answer. He wanted his family's land back, but he wasn't going to hurt her to get it. The problem was convincing her of that.

"You know . . ." He kept his voice casual, unruffled, though he felt neither. "I'm a better rancher in my sleep than Jim Horns was, or ever will be."

"But are you a better foreman?"

He smiled. "Do you mean can I take orders from a woman? If the woman knows what she's doing, yeah."

"I know what I'm doing, Will."

"I never doubted it."

She considered that for a moment before asking, "What about your job at the Lazy W?"

"I've made arrangements. My crew knows where to find me, and I'll have to check on things occasionally, but the Lazy W can manage without me for a while."

"How long?"

"However long it takes."

Again, she hesitated, and he could almost see her thoughts. She needed him, and they both knew it. The only question was whether her pride would get in the way of her admitting it.

"I can't pay you what you're making at the Lazy W," she said finally. "The ranch is free and clear, but all these accidents have hit us hard. At the moment," she hesitated, obviously embarrassed, "we're strapped for cash."

Of course, Stuart's appetite for gambling didn't help, but Will knew better than to mention that particular fact. "I'm not doing this for the money."

She looked at him, puzzled. "Why *are* you doing it?"

He hesitated, surprised and a little hurt that she needed to ask. "We're friends, Lindsey. We've been friends all our lives." He shrugged. "And friends watch out for each other."

Silence stretched out between them, long and uncertain. Again, he could see she was considering his words, questioning the truth of them. Finally, she nodded. "Okay. You're hired."

For a moment, Will found himself at a loss for words. Up until that moment, he hadn't been sure she'd accept his help. She'd always been fiercely independent, and at times it had cost her. Evidently, she'd grown up a bit.

"Good," he said, and another few moments of awkward silence followed. "I guess I better get my things stored." Standing, he started toward the door.

"One more thing, Will."

He turned back to her.

"This doesn't change anything. I mean, I'm not changing my mind about selling part of my ranch."

"That's fair."

She hesitated a moment, and then said, "I promised my father before he died that I'd keep the ranch intact."

"You don't owe me an explanation, Lindsey."

"I know, but . . . taking this job . . . you didn't owe me that either."

He nodded and again started to turn away.

"One more thing. No more . . .we can't . . ." She seemed unable to finish her sentence.

He knew what she meant but wasn't going to make it easy on her. He wanted to hear her say it. "No more what, Lindsey?"

"As you said, we're friends. And now you work for me. There's not to be any more . . ." She made a sweeping motion with her hands and settled on slipping them into the back pockets of her jeans.

"Are you saying you don't want me to kiss you again?"

She blushed but didn't look away. "Yes, that's what I'm saying."

Damn, she was something; a beautiful, stubborn woman hiding out behind denim and flannel. How had he missed it before? "Okay, I'll think about it." He turned and started toward the door before he kissed her again right there and then.

"Will . . ."

He swung back around and smiled slowly, wondering what she'd do if she could read his thoughts. Or if he acted on them. "Don't ask me to make promises I can't keep, Lindsey."

* * *

Lindsey closed her eyes and wondered if she was crazy. She felt like a spring calf who'd just invited a mountain cat to dinner. Unfortunately, she needed Will—in more ways than one.

She went to the window and watched him cross the yard toward the bunkhouse. He moved with an easy grace that never failed to stir her. With his dangerously dark eyes and a smile that could charm the devil, he'd always been too handsome for his own good.

The prospect of working with him again, seeing him day after day, frightened her. She wasn't a child any longer, with adolescent longings she didn't understand. She knew perfectly well what she wanted from Will Claxton; she just didn't know what to do about it.

She couldn't afford to turn him away.

With her finances in a mess, her brother bent on self-destruction, and someone out to ruin her, she needed a competent foreman—someone she could rely on to keep her ranch running. And one thing she was certain of was that Will Claxton knew how to run a ranch. The problem was, she still didn't trust him, though she no longer believed he'd caused the accidents plaguing her ranch. The threat he presented was more subtle and ultimately more dangerous. He wanted the Claxton Ranch, and she had no doubt he planned on getting it.

She thought of Sheriff Farley's warning. *"Be careful, Lindsey."*

Somehow, she didn't think he was referring to Will and the risk he represented.

The sight of Stuart brought her back to the present. Coming from the barn, he walked over to Will as he unloaded his truck. They stood and talked for a few minutes, and her brother didn't look pleased. Frowning, he glanced toward the house, said one last thing to Will, and headed straight for her.

She knew what was coming and, turning from the window, braced herself.

Stuart didn't disappoint her. He burst into the office seconds later full of righteous indignation. "I just talked to Will. You hired him to replace Jim Horns?"

"That's right." She crossed to her father's desk and sat down behind the massive piece of furniture. "Did *you* know Jim was looking for another job?"

The question obviously took him by surprise, and he shifted uncomfortably. "I knew he wasn't happy with the way things have been going around here."

"Who is?"

"That's not what I meant, Lindsey."

"Oh, I forgot. Jim's not concerned about some disgruntled cowboy out to ruin the Silver Creek. His problem is that women belong in the kitchen. Well, here's a newsflash for you, little brother. I can't cook."

Stuart ignored her sarcasm. Either that, or it went right over his head. "What does that have to do with Will Claxton?"

Lindsey sighed. "We were talking about replacing Jim."

"You might have at least talked to me before you made a major decision like hiring Claxton."

"Why? You usually don't care who I hire, or about anything else that goes on around here for that matter. As long as you have enough money to drink and gamble."

"That's not fair, Lindsey." His voice had taken on a definite whine. "This place is half mine."

"Not quite," she countered. "The controlling interest belongs to me." The minute the words escaped her mouth, she regretted them.

He took a step back, his expression hurt and furious.

"Stuart, I'm sorry." She moved around the desk, hand extended to her brother. "I shouldn't have said that."

"Why not?" Brushing aside her attempt to take his hand, he walked away from her. "It's the truth."

She understood why her father had left her the controlling interest in the ranch, but she'd never agreed with it. It had only increased the already large gap between her and Stuart. "If I'd known that you'd cared about my hiring Will, I'd have talked to you about it first."

He laughed bitterly. "Sure. Then you would have gone ahead and done what you wanted anyway."

Lindsey winced. He was right. "Look, Stuart—"

"Forget it, Lindsey. It's done. And you're right. I don't give a damn what you do around here."

Which was the problem, Lindsey knew. At heart, Stuart wasn't a rancher. All his life, he'd had his eye on the horizon instead of the land. Their father had never understood, and the two of them had argued constantly. Jeremiah had turned to his daughter, who loved ranching as much as he, and poured all his knowledge into her. And over the years, the gap between the two men had grown wider until they could no longer speak without harsh words passing between them. If Stuart had his way, he'd have nothing more to do with the Silver Creek.

"Buy me out and you can have it all to yourself," he said.

She sighed. "You know I don't have the cash for that."

"Then take Claxton's offer."

If only she could. If only her father hadn't tied her hands. "We've been over this before. I can't."

"Just because of some stupid promise to the old man."

She didn't expect Stuart to understand, but she'd try to explain it to him once again anyway. "This land is our heritage, Stuart."

He rolled his eyes. "Please."

"Okay, so it doesn't mean anything to you, but it meant something to Dad, and it means something to me. And on his deathbed, he made me promise—"

"Don't give me the deathbed-promise speech again. I've heard it before."

Lindsey nodded. "Then I guess there's nothing else to say."

For a moment, she and Stuart stood facing each other. Then he shook his head. "Look," he said. "I need an advance on next week's pay."

The sudden change in topic threw her. "You just got paid three days ago."

"What of it? I'm a little short."

Again, Lindsey wished she'd kept her mouth shut. She seemed to be speaking before she thought lately. Especially when dealing with her brother.

"I'm not a child, Lindsey," he said, adding to her guilt. "What I do with my money is my business. Now are you going to give me the advance or not?"

She looked at him, wishing she had the strength to turn him down. But there had been too much to deal with already today, too many encounters.

"I can give you fifty dollars," she said. "That's all the cash I have on hand."

Stuart took the money, grumbling the whole time. A few minutes later, she heard him slam the front door and start up his truck. She figured she'd be lucky if he made it back before morning.

* * *

That night, Lindsey fell into bed exhausted, fearing once again she wouldn't be able to sleep. For a while, her thoughts drifted between Will and the problems facing her ranch, but in the end, exhaustion won and sleep took over.

She dreamed of Will.

They were strolling hand in hand in a mountain meadow filled with yellow sunflowers. Their laughter floated about them, like the bright summer sunshine, and she'd never been happier. He leaned over and kissed her, a gentle brushing of his lips against hers that awakened a familiar desire inside her.

They started walking again.

All at once, Will started to run, motioning for her to race with him in the sunshine. She followed, eager to catch him. Abruptly, she stumbled, her legs giving out beneath her, and she started to fall.

"Lindsey."

His voice floated around her, calling to her. At first she reached out to him, eager to take his hand. But at the last moment she pulled back.

"Lindsey, wake up."

She struggled against the pull of his voice, not wanting this interlude to end. Finally, she opened her eyes, blinked, and closed them again.

Will leaned over her.

Strong hands on her shoulders shook her. "Come on, Lindsey, you need to wake up."

She came fully awake with a start and sat up, pulling the blankets around her. She realized he must have been trying to wake her for some time. Her cheeks heated at the memory of her dream, as if he could look into her thoughts and read them.

"What . . . what are you doing here?"

Will dragged a hand through his hair. "It's Stuart."

"Stuart." She shook her head as if to clear it. "What's he done now?"

"He's in the emergency room."

Chapter Six

W ill glanced at Lindsey, sitting ramrod straight in the passenger side of his truck. She hadn't said a dozen words since he'd woken her to tell her about Stuart, and not one since they'd started for the hospital.

"Are you okay?" he asked, fighting the urge to pull over and draw her into his arms.

Instead of answering his question, she said, "Why did the hospital call you?"

"They didn't." The question didn't surprise him. He'd known as soon as she got over the shock of hearing about Stuart, she'd start questioning the situation. "Eric called."

"Eric?"

He felt her eyes on him but kept his on the road. "The bartender at the Spur."

"I know who Eric is. What does he have to do with this?"

"He . . ." Will didn't want to say too much. He suspected that beneath her calm exterior, Lindsey held on to her emotions by a thin thread. He didn't think now was the time to find out what it would take to snap that thread. But he couldn't refuse to answer her either. "Eric took Stuart to the emergency room."

"That doesn't tell me why someone from the hospital didn't call me. What about the sheriff? Was he notified?"

"Yes, but—"

"But what? They should have called me."

Will decided he preferred her silence. It kept him from having to respond to questions he'd rather not answer—questions that would only hurt her.

"Stuart wouldn't talk to the sheriff," he said finally. "And . . ." Again, he hesitated, though he knew he couldn't lie to her. "Stuart told them not to call you."

For several long moments he could feel her eyes on him.

"Let me see if I've got this straight," she said, an edge of anger in her voice. "Someone beat up my brother badly enough to put him in the hospital. And he won't talk to the sheriff?"

Will took a deep breath. "That's about it."

She stared out the window at the dark landscape in silence.

Damn, Stuart!

If he weren't already lying in a hospital bed, Will might have been tempted to put him there. Lindsey didn't need this right now. Not with everything else she had to deal with.

Once more, he considered pulling over and trying to break through to her. She didn't have to shoulder this alone. He was here for her; she could lean on him. But again, he reined in the urge. He didn't know where these sudden impulses to comfort Lindsey came from, but he needed to keep them in check. She might be too independent for her own good, but trying to change that wasn't his job. She'd certainly made that clear enough.

Besides, he needed to remember his own reasons for helping her. Their past friendship aside, he wanted the Claxton Ranch. Sure, he could wait around until whoever was trying to force her out succeeded, but that wasn't how Will wanted to regain his family's heritage. He planned to buy the land back from Lindsey, fair and square. But first, they needed to get through this and put the Silver Creek back on stable ground.

Fifteen minutes later, he turned into the parking lot of the small regional hospital that served Willowbend and several other towns in the area.

After he parked, he turned to Lindsey. "You okay?"

God, he sounded like a broken record. But he didn't know what else to say to her. None of the old rules for dealing with her seemed to apply, and he hadn't the faintest idea what the new ones were.

Lindsey saw Will's concern and almost surrendered to it. It would be so easy—too easy—to rest her head on his shoulder and let him help carry her troubles for a while. But she'd always taken care of her own problems; her father, his hands full with handling Stuart, had expected that of her. She wasn't going to change now just because her father was no longer here to know about it.

"I'm fine," she said. It was a lie of course. She felt a lot of things right now, but fine wasn't one of them.

Will hesitated, evidently gauging her response, then nodded and climbed out of the truck.

Lindsey stayed put, resisting the need to move. On top of everything else, she hated hospitals. Especially this one.

Will opened her door, the worried expression back on his face. "Lindsey?"

Mentally shaking herself, she forced another smile and got out. "Let's go see what trouble Stuart's got himself into this time."

Inside, she steeled herself against the memories and let Will take the lead. The sharp antiseptic smell, the cold white floors, the hushed air: it all reminded her of the month she'd spent by her father's bedside. The month before he died.

Now Stuart. Although, supposedly, he was going to be okay.

Will got directions to her brother's room, and together, they made their way through the small building. She hadn't realized how much she was already leaning on Will until she stood outside Stuart's closed door.

Without looking at him she said, "Please. I need to do this alone."

"Are you sure?"

"Yes." Bracing herself, she pushed through the door into the room. She stopped short, realizing nothing could have prepared her for the sight of Stuart lying in a hospital bed.

Her father's illness had been slow, creeping up on him over a period of months. By the time he'd been hospitalized, they'd all known he didn't have long to live. But Stuart was young and vital. He didn't belong here.

Attached to a variety of tubes and monitors, he lay on his back, one arm in a cast, obviously asleep. Or unconscious. But that wasn't what tore at her heart. Other than the stark white bandage angled across one eye, Stuart's face was a swollen mass of dark bruises and angry cuts. If she hadn't known this was his room, she never would have recognized him.

"It could have been worse."

Startled, she turned toward the masculine voice. Eric,

the bartender from the Spur, sat in a dark corner behind the door.

"He's got two broken ribs and a fractured arm. And then, there's all the pretty work they did to his face."

Unsure of Eric's part in all this, she didn't respond.

Her silence didn't seem to bother him. "The good news is, there are no internal injuries. One of the ribs could have punctured a lung or something. It didn't. He was damn lucky."

Lucky? She couldn't agree with that. Not when Stuart looked like he'd been run over by a stampede. "Did you see it happen?"

"No, ma'am. I found him after. If I'd been there, it wouldn't be your brother lying in that bed." He made the statement matter-of-factly, and remembering the way he'd handled himself the other night at the Spur, Lindsey believed him.

"Where did you find him?" she asked.

She could see the hesitation on his face. He didn't want to tell her. "Please, Eric. The truth."

"In a gully. Out back of the Spur."

"Did you— Did he say who did it?"

"The boy's not talking. But I have my theories."

"So do I." She turned back to her brother. "Thank you for bringing him in."

"No problem. I'll let the two of you alone now." A moment later, she heard a soft whoosh as the door closed behind him.

Moving over to the bed, she took Stuart's hand. To her surprise, he opened his unbandaged eye.

"Lindsey." Her name came out in a whisper.

"Hey." She fought the tears clogging her voice. "I thought you were asleep."

"In and out. What are you doing here?"

"No one could have kept me away."

"I told them not to call you."

"I know." She squeezed his hand. "But this is where I belong."

He sighed and closed his eye again. "I don't want you here."

She tried to ignore the sting of his statement, but it was hard. Despite their differences, he was her brother and she loved him. "Who did this to you?" she asked before he could slip off to sleep.

Stuart shook his head. "It doesn't matter."

"Of course it matters. You can't let them get away with it. Give me a name, Stuart. Please."

He opened his eye again, and she saw the tears. "I couldn't pay them."

"This was about money?"

He laughed abruptly, as if she'd just asked the stupidest question possible. "It's always about money."

"Was it Gus? Did he and his partner do this to you?"

"You should have given me the money, Lindsey. You should have . . ."

Guilt slipped around her heart and squeezed. "I'm sorry, Stuart." A single tear slid down her face, and she brushed it away impatiently. "So sorry."

He'd closed his eye, and she didn't know whether he'd fallen asleep or just no longer wanted to look at her.

"Stuart?"

When he didn't answer, she realized he'd drifted off.

She stayed until a nurse came in to check on him. Leaving the room, Lindsey spotted Will and Eric talking in hushed tones at the end of the hall. They stopped when they noticed her approaching.

"He's asleep," she said. "The nurse said he'll be out all night."

Will brushed her cheek with the back of his fingers. "You okay?"

Again his concern threatened her control more than anything else. "I'm fine." She pressed her lips together to fight back the tears. "Stuart said it was because he couldn't pay them."

"Did he give you a name?" Eric asked.

She shook her head. "No. But I know who's responsible."

"We'll find them," Will assured her.

She nodded, her thoughts mired in guilt and self-recrimination. Where had she gone wrong? There must have been something she could have done differently to prevent Stuart from ending up like this, lying badly beaten in a hospital bed.

"Lindsey?"

Will's voice brought her out of her thoughts. "We argued this afternoon," she said, needing to explain, though Will hadn't asked. "He wanted money." She lost the battle with her tears, but she no longer cared. "I turned him down."

Will wrapped an arm around her shoulders and pulled her against his side. She didn't fight him. Instead, she buried her head against his broad chest, welcoming his strength when she knew she should be refusing. It felt good. Right. And, at the moment, she needed him.

"You can't blame yourself, Lindsey," he said softly. "Stuart got himself into this." Will's voice was seductive, soothing, weaving a spell of comfort around her.

"I should have given him the money," she said. "Then this wouldn't have happened."

"Maybe not tonight. But eventually, the gambling would have caught up with him."

Logically, she knew Will was right. This wasn't her fault.

Unfortunately, guilt paid no attention to logic. Her brother lay broken in that hospital room, and she could have prevented it by giving him the money he'd asked for.

If only she hadn't been so intent on controlling him.

Stuart was old enough to make his own decisions and live his own life. And, as he'd often pointed out, she was neither his guardian nor his parent. He'd been champing at the bit since their father's death, and she'd been attempting to rein him in tighter and tighter. No wonder he'd taken to drinking and gambling.

She had the power to set him free, to give him the one thing he wanted above all else. He hated ranching, but, in honoring her father's wishes, she'd refused to even consider buying Stuart out—even though the man holding her had offered the perfect solution. If she sold Will his family's land, she'd have the cash to buy out her brother.

"Come on, I'll take you home," Will said.

She backed out of his arms reluctantly. "No, I'm staying."

"Stuart's going to be out all night, and you need some sleep. You'll be no good to him otherwise."

Again, Will was right, though she hated admitting it. Control of her life seemed to be slipping from her grasp at an ever-accelerating speed, and she didn't know how to stop it.

"Okay," she said finally, resigned for the moment to letting Will handle things. At least to a point. "But I'll drive Stuart's truck."

Hesitating, Will threw Eric a quick glance. "His truck's not here."

Lindsey had almost forgotten about Eric but turned to him now. "Where is it?"

"We don't know," he answered. "My guess is whoever beat him up took it."

"Does the sheriff know?"

Again, the pause that told her they were keeping something from her. Looking back and forth between the two of them, she spoke very slowly, as if talking to children who didn't quite understand English. "Does the sheriff know someone stole Stuart's truck?"

Will grimaced. "Stuart says he loaned the truck to friends."

"What?" She didn't believe this. Why was her brother covering for men who'd put him in the hospital? "And, of course, he won't name those friends."

Will sighed. "You got it." He grasped her arm and gave it a reassuring squeeze. "We'll get the truck back, Lindsey. I promise."

"How? They're probably in the next county by now."

"I wouldn't be so sure about that," Eric said. "Gus isn't very bright."

"So, do you know where they are?"

Again, that silence.

"Tell me," she demanded.

Eric answered. "Gus and his pal have been hanging around the old Schaeffer place for the last week or so. They might still be out there."

Lindsey knew the place; a small, deserted ranch on the east side of town. About ten years ago, after a particularly bad winter, the Schaeffers had just picked up and left. As far as Lindsey knew, no one had heard from them since.

"You're going out there, aren't you." It wasn't a question, though when neither one answered, she said, "What is this?" She glanced from one man to the other. "Some kind of male code of silence? My brother's in that hospital bed, and you two are like a couple of closed-mouthed old hens. I want to know what's going on."

Will sighed and slipped his hands into the back pockets of his jeans. "We thought we'd go have a look around. See if Stuart's truck is out there."

"And rough up Gus and company in the process?" Lindsey added.

Will didn't answer, but he didn't have to. She knew Will Claxton and his overblown sense of honor, and Eric seemed no better. They weren't going to let this go, not as long as they thought they knew who had beaten up Stuart.

"Take me with you," she demanded.

"No."

"I'm going."

"It's not a good idea, Lindsey," Eric added. "You—"

She cut him off, speaking directly to Will. "Take me with you, or I'll find a way to get out there myself."

Will cursed and looked away.

She moved in a little closer, forcing him to look at her. "You know I'll do it, Will Claxton. I'll find a way out there. With or without the two of you."

After a moment he looked at Eric. "We better take her." Eric shook his head and started to say something, but Will interrupted. "She'll be safer with us."

Eric frowned but shrugged in resignation. "It's your show."

Lindsey took a deep breath. For the first time in several days, she felt like she had regained some measure of control. She was going after the men who'd hurt her brother and stolen his property. And she was going to make sure they didn't get away with it.

* * *

No one spoke as they made their way out to the Schaeffer place, but Will was intensely aware of Lindsey sitting beside him. Her presence taunted him. The long, slender length of her thighs stretched out next to his, touching his only when an occasional bump or turn tossed them together, or the movement of an arm, hers or his, caused one to brush against the other; each was a reminder of the danger of having her along.

Contrary to what she thought, he and Eric were going to retrieve Stuart's truck. Nothing else. They'd let the sheriff handle the rest. But with a man like Gus, things could get out of hand real quick, and Will didn't want to have to worry about Lindsey's safety.

If he thought it would do any good, he'd try again to talk her out of this, but he knew he'd be wasting his breath. With Lindsey, reason didn't always work. She was the most stubborn woman he'd ever known. He had no doubt she would have made good on her threat if he'd left her behind. She would have found a way to follow them. God only knew what trouble she'd have gotten herself into then. At least this way, he could keep an eye on her.

Somehow, that thought wasn't very comforting.

It seemed to take hours, but finally, they arrived at the Schaeffers' deserted ranch. Will slowed the truck and shut off the lights.

In the dark, with only a half-moon providing light, the house and barn appeared well tended. But as they drew closer, the deterioration and neglect became evident. A fence fallen in disrepair, the barn door hanging half off its hinges, the windows of the house broken, glass shattered and lying in pools that caught and reflected the moonlight: it was a sad fate for what had once been someone's home. Someone's life.

Then Will saw the truck.

"That's it," Lindsey whispered at the same moment. "Next to the house."

"I think you're right." Will looked around for Gus and his pal, knowing they wouldn't have gone off and left their prize. "Now, where are—"

"There they are," Eric said. Gus and his friend ambled out onto the dilapidated porch of the house with two women behind them. "Looks like they heard us coming."

Will stopped the truck and switched on his headlights, framing Gus and his friends in the glare. "But not soon enough."

Both men were bootless and half-dressed, with unbuttoned shirts hastily thrown on. The women were in even more disarray.

Eric reached for the shotgun on the rack behind him, but Will said, "Leave it. They're not armed. Let's not ask for more trouble than necessary."

Eric seemed to hesitate but finally nodded. "As I said, this is your show."

Will opened the door. To Lindsey, he said, "Stay here." Then he and Eric climbed out of the truck.

"Well, well," Gus said, as he slipped an arm around one of the women. "If it isn't the cowboy hero. And . . ." He swayed a bit and gave a mocking, half bow toward Eric. "His faithful companion. Where's your shotgun, bartender?"

"Don't need it for the likes of you."

"Oooh. He do talk big, don't he, honey?"

The woman giggled but looked nervous.

Will didn't blame her. Gus was obviously drunk, and violence hovered about him like clouds before a storm.

"Look who else is here," said Gus's partner, Ray.

Gus broke into a drunken grin. "Well, well. If it isn't the little ball-breaker herself."

Will glanced back as Lindsey walked up behind them. "Dammit, Lindsey. I told you to stay in the truck."

"You didn't really think I would, did you?"

No. He should have known she'd ignore his command to stay put. She was the most bull-headed . . .

"You coming to see what you missed, sweet thing?" Gus laughed and grabbed his crotch in an obscene gesture.

"Why you filthy . . ." Will started forward.

Eric stopped him with a hand on his arm. "Easy, Will. That's not what we're here for."

Evidently undeterred by Gus' taunts, Lindsey stepped up beside Will. "I came for my brother's truck."

"Your brother's truck?" Gus glanced innocently at the black pickup. "Is that your brother's truck?"

Lindsey glared at the man.

Will had to admire her courage, although he seethed over her foolishness. Gus was dangerous, and Will suspected he'd like nothing better than to teach Lindsey his own, very unpleasant, lesson about male-female roles.

"Well, I guess it is Stuart's heap at that," Gus sneered. "But as you can see, we're using it right now."

"Not anymore." Lindsey started toward the truck, but Will grabbed her arm.

"That's enough, Lindsey," he said. "This isn't the Silver Creek." And Gus wasn't a hired hand she could bully into submission.

"Better listen to him, sweet thing." Gus let go of the woman at his side and leaned down to pick up something from the porch. "'Cause I'm in a real mean mood."

Will's blood ran cold at the sight of the tire iron in Gus's hand. Releasing Lindsey's arm, he shoved her behind him. "Get her out of here, Eric."

"Yeah, bartender. Run and hide," snickered Gus as he stepped down from the porch. "We'll come find you later. After we take care of the hero here."

"I wouldn't be so sure of that if I were you." Will side-stepped and started to circle the other man, drawing his attention away from Lindsey and Eric. "I put you on your back once. I can do it again."

"Okay, tough guy, let's go."

Out of the corner of his eye, Will saw Eric grab Lindsey and head toward his truck. She wasn't going easy, but Eric didn't give an inch. Good thing, Will thought, because he didn't have time to worry about her. Right now, he needed all his wits to defend himself against that tire iron.

Then Gus's pal hit Eric like a runaway bronc, knocking him to the ground. Free of his grip, Lindsey back-stepped as the two men tumbled to the ground, a mass of flying fists. Will cursed, but came back to his own situation in time to duck as Gus came at him, swinging the metal club.

The brush of cold steel just missed his cheek as Will dove for Gus's knees, grateful for the liquor slowing the other man's responses. The two of them went down, falling back against the rotting railing that gave way beneath their weight, and the tire iron flew from Gus's hand.

A woman screamed.

Lindsey?

Will swiveled toward Eric, who still struggled with Ray, but didn't see her. A sharp pain slammed through his head as Gus's fist connected with his jaw. Will forced himself to forget about Lindsey and concentrate on the man who seemed intent on killing him.

Together, they rolled amid the shards of broken glass and splintered wood littering the sagging porch. A mad drunk and an ex-marine with a score to settle. Gus had size and weight on his side, but the liquor slowed him. Will had only his anger and his determination not to let this man anywhere near Lindsey Baker.

He figured that made them just about even.

Finally, Will got enough leverage to deliver a full punch, and Gus sagged against the ground. Breathing heavily, Will struggled to his feet and backed up, his thoughts shifting immediately to Lindsey. Where was—

A fraction too late he saw the ragged piece of broken railing that slammed into his head, knocking him to his knees. His vision blurred, the pain tearing through his head, threatening to shatter his grip on consciousness.

He fought it, while as if in a dream, he saw Gus drop the wood and scramble for the tire iron.

Will had to get on his feet. Had to move. Or he was a dead man. And then Lindsey—

A gunshot split the air.

Chapter Seven

Will staggered to his feet and pivoted on unsteady legs toward the shot.

Lindsey lowered the gun she'd fired into the air and took up a shooter's stance. Backlit by the truck's lights, she looked like an avenging angel, all fiery red hair and steely resolve, as she aimed the .45 revolver at Gus.

Will shook his head, but it was his anger that cleared his sight. The damn woman was going to get herself killed.

"Back off," she said, her voice as cool and hard as the weapon in her hand.

"Or what?" Gus gripped the tire iron in his right hand, grinning like a madman. "You gonna shoot me?"

She cocked the hammer. "It's a thought."

Gus snorted. "You better put that thing down, sweetheart, before you hurt yourself."

Will moaned. Gus was either too drunk or too stupid for words. There was nothing hesitant or unsure about Lindsey's posture, nothing hinting at a bluff. Besides, Will had seen her shoot. He might be angry at her for not staying in the truck, but he had no doubt Lindsey could handle that gun. *But where the hell had she gotten it?*

"This is your last warning, Gus." Lindsey spit out his name like a curse.

"You don't scare me, bitch." Still grinning, Gus took a step forward, wielding the tire iron like a threat. "You ain't got what it takes to shoot a man."

She pulled the trigger, and the tire iron leaped into the air as the bullet grazed the back of Gus's fist.

With a howl of pain, he folded in half, cradling his bleeding hand. "You shot me. I can't believe you shot me."

Lindsey lowered her aim. "How about a kneecap next?"

"You're crazy. You know that?" Still bent at the waist, Gus raised his uninjured arm and backed up. "Crazy!"

Will fought a grin. Damn, she was something.

How could he continue to be angry at her? She was a fascinating combination of tomboy and woman, soft curves and feminine grace with an iron will and the courage to back it. He realized this was what had always drawn him to Lindsey.

From that time in first grade when she'd taken a swing at him, her red braids flying, this scintillating combination of femininity and strength had intrigued and bewitched him. Strange that it had taken him all these years to recognize it.

Moving on shaky legs to her side, he reached for the .45. "He's done for, Lindsey. Give me the gun."

"Like hell, you can hardly stand. I'm surprised you're even conscious considering the blow you took."

Will reached up and tentatively explored the gash on his head. He'd been so preoccupied, he hadn't even realized he was bleeding. "I guess that's why my vision's a little fuzzy."

She let out a short, humorless laugh and shook her head. "You always were hardheaded, Claxton. Get in Stuart's truck. I'm driving."

"Eric!" she called, keeping her eyes and the gun on Gus. "You got Ray taken care of?"

Will had forgotten about the other two men. Glancing at them, he saw Eric had a chokehold on Gus's partner.

"Everything's under control here," Eric said blandly.

"Good. Take Will's truck," Lindsey ordered. "Someone will pick it up in the morning."

"You got it." Eric released Ray and shoved him toward Gus. "What about our friends here? We just going to leave them?"

"Stop by the sheriff's office when you get back to town," Will said. "Let him know what happened out here."

"Tell him I'll be in tomorrow to file charges," Lindsey added.

"Charges!" Gus took a step forward but quickly backed up again as Lindsey re-aimed the .45. "I'll tell you about filing charges, bitch." He waved his bloody hand in her direction. "You shot me. There's a law against *that*."

Will walked the few feet to the tire iron lying in the dust and picked it up. "How about it, Lindsey? You think this might be the weapon used to break Stuart's ribs?"

"Could be."

Then Will moved to the broken porch and, after a moment's search, grabbed a jagged piece of wood with a nail protruding from the end. "And if Stuart doesn't remember who assaulted him, I bet the blood on the end of this piece matches mine."

"Don't forget auto theft." She nodded toward the black truck. "That's Silver Creek property, and I'm controlling partner." Smiling, she cocked her head as if in thought. "And I don't remember loaning it to anyone."

"Why you—" Gus started.

Will raised a hand palm out. "I wouldn't if I were you." Nodding toward Lindsey, he said, "She's got a real bad temper."

Gus settled back, and Will returned to Lindsey's side.

"Eric, tell the sheriff that Lindsey and I will be in tomorrow to answer any questions." To Lindsey, he said, "If you're going to drive, you need to give me that gun. You can't do both."

For a moment, she looked like she was seriously considering trying. Fortunately, she conceded. "Okay," she said. "Take it. But don't let him out of your sights."

"Yes, ma'am," he replied, his voice dripping with sarcasm. "I'll do my best."

Lindsey threw him a poisonous glance, but handed him the weapon.

Just as he started to get into the truck, he remembered the two women who'd been with Gus and his pal. Looking around, Will spotted them hovering inside the run-down house. With the mood Gus was in, Will couldn't leave them behind.

"If you ladies need a ride into town," he called, "you best climb on in the back there." He nodded toward his truck with Eric in the driver's seat.

The two women glanced nervously at Gus and Ray, and, not surprisingly, hurried out of the house and followed Will's advice.

"Okay," Will said. "Let's go."

As Lindsey drove away, he watched Gus out the back window, knowing this wasn't over.

* * *

Lindsey tried not to look at Will on the drive back to the Silver Creek. She failed miserably. Every few minutes, she found herself glancing over, just to make sure he was okay. He sat with his eyes closed and his head back against the seat, holding a rag against his forehead. The bleeding appeared to have stopped, but the cut worried her.

"You need to see a doctor," she said again. "Let me take you back to the emergency room."

"It looks worse than it is." Will repeated the same words he'd spoken moments earlier. "Head wounds always bleed heavily, Lindsey. You know that."

Yes, she knew that. Around the ranch, she'd seen quite a few similar injuries, but at the moment, her thought processes were anything but logical. A myriad of emotions swirled inside her, each warring for dominance over the other. She couldn't remember ever having been this angry. Or frightened.

She was angry at Stuart for starting this whole mess and at Will for carrying it further—angry because they both had frightened her. When she'd first heard about Stuart in the hospital, it had taken all her willpower to hold herself together. Then Gus had swung that tire iron at Will's head, and her heart had seemed to stop.

Lord only knew what would have happened if Will hadn't ducked. Or if she hadn't remembered the gun stashed away in Stuart's truck. Most likely, Will would be suffering from more than a gash to his head. He might be—

She stopped that thought and glanced over at him, resisting the urge to suggest again that they head back to town. Will had decided he didn't need to see a doctor, and she knew him well enough to realize he wasn't going to change his mind.

A few minutes later, she pulled into the yard of the Silver Creek and parked in front of the house. Turning to Will, she said, "Since you're being stubborn about seeing a doctor, you're stuck with letting me tend that cut."

"It's nothing. It'll be—"

"Don't argue with me, Will." She climbed out of the truck. Looking back at him, she added, "I'm not in the mood for any more heroics. Come inside." She slammed the door and started toward the house.

She didn't know if he'd follow, or ignore her and head on out to the bunkhouse. Stubborn might be his middle name, but if he defied her on this, she'd teach him a whole new meaning of the word. Just about the time she figured she'd have to go after him, he entered the kitchen.

Relieved, she turned to the stove. "Have a seat," she said without looking at him. "I'll just get this coffee started, and then I'll see to that cut." She heard the scrape of wood against wood as he pulled a chair away from the table. "I hope you don't mind, the coffee's left over from this morning."

"Just so long as it's hot and strong."

"It could probably walk on its own." Forcing a smile, she turned, her next words dying in her throat as the kitchen light revealed her first good look at his injury. She should have ignored his protests and taken him to the emergency room. The ragged gash looked angry and painful and probably needed stitches.

"Lindsey?"

The question in his voice made her realize she'd been staring. Without answering him, she headed out of the kitchen. She needed a moment or two alone to come to terms with a few things.

"Where are you going?"

She stopped in the doorway, momentarily frozen. Then, embarrassed, she got control of herself and said, "I'll be right back. I need to get something for that thick skull of yours."

Alone in the bathroom, she wrapped her arms around her middle as her stomach knotted.

She'd almost lost him.

In the kitchen, that knowledge had hit her with force, frightening her more than she'd thought possible.

Will had always been a part of her life. Even during the years he'd been away, though angry and hurt by his silence, she'd thought of him as her best friend. Since his return, she'd always known where to find him. He'd always been within reach if she'd wanted or needed him. She'd never before faced the possibility that some day she might lose him forever.

Damn him!

She'd never asked to care this much about Will Claxton, didn't want to, in fact. Evidently, she had no choice. All her life, she'd had strong feelings for him which he'd never returned. It looked like some things hadn't changed.

The only question left was what she was going to do about it.

One thing she knew for certain, she couldn't let him know how much he meant to her. His family's land was too important to him, more important than their friendship. Besides, he'd already proven he wasn't above using her reactions to him to his advantage.

Pulling herself together, she opened the medicine cabinet.

The best thing would be for her to go on as though

nothing had happened, like she hadn't even noticed how close he'd come to losing his life. She would treat his injuries and send him on his way. All easier said than done. Especially when she still quaked inside and her hands wouldn't stop trembling.

A few moments later, she made her way back to the kitchen with an armload of first-aid supplies. Eyes closed, Will had pushed his chair back on its hind legs to lean against the wall.

Fear turned her stomach. "Are you okay?"

He opened his eyes and smiled, a slow, sexy smile that sent shivers of awareness down her spine. "Except for a killer headache, I've never been better."

Fear wasn't something she'd had much experience with, and she didn't like it. She concentrated instead on her anger. It was a familiar emotion; one she could control.

"Serves you right." She set a bottle of aspirin on the table in front of him. "After pulling that kind of stunt."

"Stunt?" He laughed abruptly. "You mean getting Stuart's truck back?"

"You know exactly what I mean." She went to the sink, her hands shaking as she filled a water glass and handed it to him for the pills.

"I was just doing my job."

"Your job? Funny—" She crossed her arms and locked gazes with him. "I don't remember including 'retrieve stolen property' in your job description."

He grinned. "I don't have a job description."

She didn't dignify that with a response.

"Okay," he said, somewhat mollified. "I didn't think you could afford to lose that truck."

He was right, but she'd be damned before she'd admit it.

Turning back to the sink, she filled a bowl with warm

water. "You should have let the sheriff handle it instead of racing off like some kind of hero."

"Don't get all huffy on me, Lindsey."

"Huffy!" She spun back around to face him.

"You wanted a piece of Gus as badly as I did."

That stopped her. She couldn't deny it. When she thought of what Gus and Ray had done to her brother, she saw red. "Maybe."

"No maybe about it. You enjoyed every minute while holding that gun on him." The two front legs of his chair hit the floor with a thud. "I told you to stay in the truck where you'd be safe. Did it ever occur to you that *you* could have been hurt?"

She heard the anger in his voice, and it surprised her. He knew she could take care of herself. Besides, she'd been the one with the gun. "I had to stop the fight before he killed you."

"Before he killed me?" He laughed briefly and without humor. Then he shook his head. "I didn't know you cared."

She turned back to the sink to gather what she needed to clean and treat his forehead. "Yeah, well, we all have our moments of stupidity."

"Where did you get it?"

"Where did I get what?"

"The gun."

"Oh." She hesitated, not because she didn't want to tell him, but because of the way he was looking at her, unnerving her as he always did with those eyes of his. "Stuart keeps it under the front seat of his truck."

She stepped up next to him. "Now can we get this over with?" Just the thought of touching him disturbed her.

"Be my guest."

She forced herself into action. "Hold still." Her voice

sounded harsher than she'd intended, but somehow, it managed to get her moving. Trying not to think of the feel of his hair beneath her fingers, she parted his hair and started cleaning the gash.

Will sucked in his breath.

"Don't be a baby," she snapped, but gentled her touch.

Will held perfectly still as Lindsey edged closer. She seemed totally unaware of her effect on him, of the fact that her knees brushed his thighs and her breasts swayed dangerously near his face. Closing his eyes, he focused on the feel of her hands instead.

That wasn't much better.

She surrounded him like a warm summer night, her touch, her scent, her heat. He couldn't understand why he'd never noticed these things about her before. Had he been blind? And why now—when neither one of them needed or wanted this type of distraction—couldn't he get her out of his head?

He tried concentrating on the feel of her cleaning the cut on his head. She was efficient but gentle. But his thoughts shifted, and he no longer thought about her tending his injuries. Instead, he imagined those same hands on his body. Against his bare chest. Down his back. Wrapped around his . . .

He opened his eyes and looked into her startled green ones.

She went utterly still, and for a moment, he thought she'd read his mind. Then he was certain of it as she quickly finished dressing his wound, and then backed away. He grabbed her wrist, halting her escape. Bringing her hand to his face, he kissed her palm. He heard her sharp intake of breath and smiled to himself.

She felt it too—this crazy desire neither of them could deny.

"Where have you been hiding all my life?" he asked thickly, hardly recognizing his own voice.

"I've always been here." Her voice, too, sounded different, soft and utterly alluring.

"I've never met you before." He tightened his hold on her wrist, watching her as he again brushed his lips against her skin.

"You just never saw me."

"That's not true. You're not the Lindsey Baker I know." He wanted her. God, how he wanted her. "You're someone else. Someone new."

It was the wrong thing to say. He saw it in her eyes as she seemed to come back to herself and slip away from him, mentally and physically taking a step backward.

Will couldn't let her go. Not yet.

Grabbing her other arm, he stopped her, pulling her onto his lap.

"Will—" she started.

"Shh . . ." He wrapped one arm around her waist and, brushing her hair aside, nuzzled the side of her neck. "Maybe it's me who's different. Maybe I'm the one who's not the same."

"You're tired. You need to rest."

He kissed her neck lightly, tasting her skin, relishing its softness. He felt the shudder go through her, and he hardened in response. "No, I don't think rest is what I need. What either of us needs."

"You promised you wouldn't touch me."

"Did I?" He followed the line of her neck with his mouth, pushing the top of her shirt aside to caress the arc of her shoulder. "I don't remember."

"Yes." Her voice was little more than a breathless whisper. "You did."

"I didn't mean it." He nipped her gently. "Did you?"

She didn't answer but made no move to pull away from him. Instead, she bent her head to give him better access, while her hands gripped the arm around her waist.

"You taste so good, Lindsey." He shifted and raised a hand to her face, to caress her cheek with the back of his fingers. "So good." He urged her head forward, and she whimpered as his lips touched hers.

"Kiss me back," he whispered against her mouth. "I want you to kiss me." He brushed his tongue against her lips, once, twice. "Please."

In answer, she opened her mouth, letting him deepen the kiss, responding to him like she'd done the day on the ledge. He held her tightly, one arm about her waist, while moving his other hand to the buttons of her shirt.

The hiss of steaming liquid shattered the stillness.

Lindsey jerked away from him, standing in one fluid motion, though her legs appeared unsteady. Her hands flew to the unfastened buttons of her shirt, and she hurried over to the stove, turned it off, and started fussing with the coffeepot and mugs.

Will stood and crossed the room to stand behind her.

She must have sensed him, because suddenly she went very still. "I guess it's a little late for coffee," she said shakily.

"It's not coffee either of us wants."

"You should leave, Will."

Reaching around her, he removed the mug from her hand and placed it back on the counter. Gently, he turned her to face him, lifting her chin with one finger. He had to know the truth about where he stood with her, whether this was all him, or if she felt it too. Everything was there in her eyes: her desire, her fear, her vulnerability.

"If that's what you want, I'll go."

For a moment she didn't answer, her eyes wide. Then suddenly, she seemed to surrender, to him or herself he couldn't say.

"No." She rested a hand against his chest. "I want you to stay."

Will covered her hand with his, but made no further move. He wouldn't push her further, couldn't. It had to be her decision.

She took a step closer, and he lowered his hands to her waist. She raised up on her toes and kissed him, as lightly as he'd kissed her earlier. He tightened his hold on her, drawing her closer until the entire length of their bodies pressed together. "Take me upstairs, Will."

Chapter Eight

Lindsey couldn't say exactly when she'd decided to stop fighting—herself and Will. But at some point, it was no longer a question of right or wrong, or whether she cared too much for a man who wanted something she couldn't give.

It simply became a matter of need.

A need she'd felt for him since the first awakening of her womanhood. A need she'd hidden and tried to satisfy with other men. A need to make love with Will Claxton at least once in her life.

Beneath her hand, his heart beat steadily while his dark, hungry eyes searched hers. For the moment at least, she knew he wanted her. That would have to be enough. She stepped forward, bringing her body closer to his.

"Please, Will," she repeated. "Take me upstairs."

He studied her for a moment longer, then leaned over and kissed her, longer and deeper than before, his tongue exploring her mouth with a thoroughness that stole her breath. When he finally broke away, a dark smile crept up his face, a smile filled with heat and desire, and the promise of passion.

He took her hand, and she followed him as he made his way unerringly through her silent house. It felt strange and yet infinitely familiar to be with him like this, her hand in his with the thought of making love in both their minds.

As they were growing up, Will had spent more time here than in his own home. She couldn't count the number of hours they'd passed together in her room, sharing their lives. Their hopes and dreams. Their fears. Now they had a different agenda, one she'd kept close to her heart through all those years. One she'd only dared wish for in the deepest, most private corners of her soul. One she'd never told anyone, not even Will. Especially not Will.

Inside her room, he stopped and turned to her, and she saw the question in his eyes, those wonderfully sensuous eyes of his that had never looked at her in quite this way before. He was putting aside his own desires and giving her one last chance to change her mind.

It made her want him all the more.

Closing the distance between them, she answered his unspoken question by wrapping her arms around his neck and brushing her lips lightly against his. Will instantly deepened the kiss and slid his hands down her sides to grasp her hips and draw her fully against his arousal. She'd waited half her life for this, and she responded with all the passion of her suppressed emotions. Winding her fingers into his hair, she held him close, matching the demands of his mouth with her own.

She would have this night. And she would have her memories.

He broke the kiss, and she whimpered softly.

"Patience," he whispered as his deft fingers made short

work of her buttons. He tugged the shirt off her shoulders and down her arms, replacing the fabric with his mouth.

She held on to him, her head thrown back as the delicious sensations rippled across her skin and settled in the lower part of her body.

Will sighed as he kissed her.

She had the softest skin, scented with baby powder and the heady smell of a woman. He ran his tongue over her collarbone and nibbled gently at her shoulder, while his hands explored her nipples beneath the fabric of her white cotton bra.

He couldn't help but smile.

He hadn't expected her to wear silk or satin, but he never would have guessed that cotton could be so sexy. So completely decadent. Through the material, he rubbed her nipples, plucking them until they rose to hard peaks. He heard her moan, deep in her throat, and she grabbed onto his waist.

Another surprise. This hidden passion of hers that sent desire racing through him like a prairie fire out of control.

He backed her up, one step, two, until the back of her legs struck the bed. Lowering her onto the mattress, he continued his exploration, running his lips from her neck to the sweet mounds of her breasts and back again to the base of her throat.

Her chest was lightly freckled, and he could have spent hours kissing each lovely spot in turn. Instead, his hands seemed to move of their own accord to unfasten her bra and push it aside. As the cool air hit her already aroused nipples, they tightened further, and he shifted so he could see her.

"You're beautiful," he whispered, unable to take his eyes off her. She had small, perfectly formed breasts that responded to his lightest touch. He stroked her, gently toying with the pebbled centers. "So beautiful."

She blushed prettily, and he had to taste her.

He took first one breast and then the other into his mouth, lavishing attention on each until she moaned beneath him.

Her hands, on his back and in his hair, urged him on and begged for more. Unable to deny either of them, he rose up on one arm. Lindsey yanked his shirt from the waistband of his jeans and nearly ripped the buttons in her haste to rid him of the garment.

Reclaiming her mouth, he pushed her back onto the mattress and shifted on top of her. The sensation of bare skin against bare skin sent fresh waves of hunger through him.

He'd never wanted a woman this badly, never experienced this raw, urgent need to possess and be possessed, and he didn't understand it. All he knew was that he ached to be in her, to feel her moist heat close around him.

Without breaking the kiss, he fumbled with her belt buckle and the snap and zipper of her jeans. He felt clumsy and inexperienced, like a teenager on hormonal overdrive.

Once he got her jeans unfastened, he released her mouth, and Lindsey kicked off her boots and lifted her hips so he could peel the denim off her long slender legs. Then they both went to work ridding him of his clothes.

Finally, there was nothing left between them, and he forced himself to slow down, to draw back and look at her. She was like a mountain cat, all sleek muscle and graceful curves. He touched her gently, reverently, skimming his hands down from the base of her neck to the top of her thighs and back again.

He realized that he'd been wrong earlier when he

claimed not to know her. He recognized everything about her, her long slender body, the freckles sprinkled across her chest, the paleness of her skin. Even her passion—he'd seen it a hundred, no, a thousand times before in her fierce independence and the way she threw herself into things. Lindsey was one of a kind, and he knew her better than he'd ever known another woman.

Yet there was this side of her that he'd never seen before. He never would have guessed that she'd respond to his lightest touch, or that she'd make him want to bury himself in her forever and never let her go.

"God, Lindsey." In her hot green eyes, he saw a reflection of his own confusion and need. He caressed her cheek with the back of his fingers. "I don't understand this." He shook his head, bewildered by the passion that had erupted between them. "Where did it come from?"

She lifted up and brushed her lips along the base of his throat, her mouth like a cooling balm against the heat of his skin. "Does it matter?"

He lowered his head and kissed her slowly, gently. Then he pulled back again. "Yes, it matters. A great deal."

Lindsey reached up and stroked his cheek like he'd done hers. She'd always known making love to Will would be wonderfully passionate. She'd just never expected this gentleness.

It broke her heart.

She couldn't fool herself. There was no future for them, nothing more than this one night. On Will's part, their love-making probably had more to do with residual energy from the danger they'd faced than any romantic feelings toward her. Oh, she knew he cared for her as a friend, but that was a long way from building a future together. Besides, he'd walked out on her before, never giving their friendship a second thought, and she couldn't be sure he wouldn't do the same thing again.

Tomorrow or the next day, he'd realize his mistake, and, if they were lucky, their relationship would return to what it had been before they'd slept together. If they weren't so lucky, Lindsey would lose his friendship as well.

As for her feelings, well . . .

She'd have this one night, these memories. It would have to be enough.

"Finish it, Will." She reached up and nipped at his mouth. "Make love to me."

Deepening the kiss, he moved his hand to the inside of her thighs. Lindsey gasped and arched against his touch, and the gentleness gave way to urgency. He moved on top of her, pinned her beneath him, and spread her legs with his knees.

Then he pulled back just enough so she could see his face, his eyes, and Lindsey found herself caught by the swirl of passion in their dark depths. Then he slid inside her, and she could think of nothing except how much she loved this man, how much she had always loved him. And how much harder it was going to be *now* to give him up again.

As the first gray fingers of dawn crept around the edges of her windows, Lindsey watched Will sleep. He looked so peaceful, so unlike the vibrant man she knew. It was another side of him, and like everything else about him, it tugged at her heart, making her wish things could be different between them.

"Good morning."

His voice brought her out of her thoughts. "I thought you were sleeping."

"Not anymore." Reaching up, he pulled her down for a lingering good-morning kiss that left her aching for more.

He released her too soon and said, "I should go."

She circled his neck with her arms and snuggled closer. "Do you have to?"

He smiled, a slow, sexy smile that warmed her heart and sent fresh shivers of desire through her. "Unless you want every cowhand on this ranch to know where I spent the night, yeah, I think I do."

Lindsey groaned. What had she been thinking? Of course he had to leave. She should have sent him packing hours ago. "You're right. You'd better go."

He kissed her again, thoroughly this time, before rolling off the bed to gather up his clothes. "I'll clean up down at the bunkhouse."

"Will . . ." Suddenly, the implications of his arriving back at the barn just after dawn struck her. Especially if anyone saw him coming from the main house.

It wasn't that she was ashamed of sleeping with Will. Her personal life was no one's business but her own. But she was a woman running a ranch—a world dominated by cowboys who still believed women belonged barefoot, pregnant, and in the kitchen. She'd worked hard to earn the respect of her men. If it got out she was sleeping with her foreman, she'd be the butt of jokes that could destroy that respect in a heartbeat.

"Don't worry, Lindsey." Again, Will's voice broke into her thoughts. "No one will know where I've been."

She sank back onto the bed, embarrassed that she'd been so transparent.

Will started toward the door and stopped. Without looking at her, he said, "This isn't over, you know."

"Will, we can't—"

He cut her off with a look. "Yes, we can."

He held her gaze, his eyes dark and dangerous, and for a moment, he seemed like a total stranger. Suddenly, he smiled, winked, and it was Will again. Her Will.

"Just try and keep me away."

Then he was gone.

* * *

After Will left, Lindsey stalled.

For once, she was in no hurry to start the endless chores that made up her day. Instead, she took her time cleaning up, dressing, and forcing herself to eat. Even knowing Will was the reason for her sudden reluctance to head outside didn't make it any easier.

Despite her resolve to settle for the one night, the hours spent in Will's arms were playing havoc on her thoughts— not to mention her emotions. Her mood swung dramatically between delicious memories and an irrational fear of facing him in the bright light of day. She worried that he'd see her differently. And, that he wouldn't.

By the time she finally made it out to the yard, Will had gotten her crew started on the last of the branding. She watched his easy camaraderie with her men and envied it. With her, there was always an awareness that she wasn't one of the crew. Whether it was because of her gender or simply because she owned the ranch, she didn't know. But Will faced neither obstacle, and no one seemed the least disturbed by the change from one foreman to the other. But then, most of her crew had known Will all their lives, and those who hadn't, knew his reputation.

When he spotted her, he started toward the fence where she stood watching.

She had to admit he looked great.

There was nothing unusual in that, but how a man could look that good wearing a pair of well-worn jeans and a cotton work shirt was beyond her. Of course, it didn't hurt the way those jeans fit, molding themselves to his muscled thighs and lean hips like they'd been made for him. It reminded her of the way he'd looked the night before, wearing nothing.

"I almost hate to interrupt those thoughts," he drawled as he came to a stop in front of her. "They look positively X-rated."

A flush of heat touched her cheeks, and she realized she needed to get control of her wayward thoughts. Glancing around quickly to see if anyone else had heard him, she said, "Will, this isn't—"

"Don't worry, Linds. No one's paying any attention to us."

"But . . ." she started to warn him, then decided it was best to just change the subject. Nodding toward the branding crew, she said, "It looks like you have everything under control."

Will grinned, and she suspected he knew what she was trying to do. For the moment, he went along with it. "You have a good crew."

It took her a moment, but she smiled at the compliment. "What's left of it."

"Looks to me like the shake-up may have been a good thing. It left you with only the better hands. The others took off."

"The silver lining?"

He shrugged. "Maybe."

Small talk. Once they'd exhausted it, an awkward silence took over. She searched for something to break it.

"How's your head?" she asked finally.

"I'll survive. Thanks to a half-dozen aspirin, and"—he touched the bandage under his hat—"excellent medical care."

Again, she chose to ignore his innuendo. "I hope you're taking it easy. I'd hate for that thing to open up again. It would—" Realizing she was rambling, she stopped herself.

"Then you'd have to treat it all over again."

She saw the memories in his eyes, and, again, heat touched her cheeks. They couldn't do this. She couldn't do this. Not here. And not now.

Turning away from him, she said, "Since everything seems under control, I'm going to head into town. I want to talk to the sheriff and go see Stuart."

"Give me a few minutes, and I'll go with you."

"There's no reason for both of us to go."

"I'm going. These men don't need me looking over their shoulders."

She knew there was no point in arguing with him. Especially since the real reason she wanted to go alone was that she wanted some time away from him. Away from the constant reminder of the night before. Of course, she couldn't tell him that.

Besides, she suspected he already knew.

* * *

As Will had expected, the ride to town was tense.

He knew why Lindsey had wanted to do this alone, and

it had nothing to do with one of them staying behind to tend the ranch. She didn't want to think about what had happened between them, and she certainly didn't want to talk about it.

Will wasn't going to let her get away with either. Their relationship had taken a sharp detour last night, a turn that had nothing, and everything, to do with their making love. At some point, protecting Lindsey had become more important than regaining his family's land, and making love to her more imperative than his next breath. He didn't understand any of it, and that scared him more than anything. Sooner or later, they *would* talk. But not now. Not until they'd settled a few things with Gus and Stuart. Not until Will had a little more time to think things through.

Meanwhile, he was very aware of her in the small space.

Unlike last night, she sat as far away from him as possible, almost hugging the passenger door. He would have thought the distance would make a difference. It didn't.

He could no longer think of Lindsey the way he had as little as twenty-four hours ago. Looking at her, he saw the woman he'd come to know last night, the woman hidden beneath the denim and tough-girl attitude.

He remembered everything . . .

The smell of baby powder—soft, feminine, and deceptively innocent. The feel of her skin, smooth and slick beneath his hands. The taste of her lips and the sound of her moans. The sight of her eyes, those bright green eyes, clouded with passion. And her fiery red hair, tangled in his fists as he thrust into her.

She could keep her distance all she wanted. It no longer mattered. He wasn't likely to forget anything about her any time soon.

* * *

They stopped first at the sheriff's office.

Eric had filled the sheriff in the night before, and the two of them had ridden out to the Schaeffer Ranch this morning. To no one's surprise, Gus and Ray were long gone.

It didn't matter anyway.

Unless Lindsey could convince Stuart to name the men who'd beaten him up, the sheriff's hands were tied. He couldn't issue a warrant for assault if the injured party refused to file a complaint. And as for auto theft, Stuart had claimed he'd lent his truck to Gus.

Of course, Will could file charges, but the sheriff advised against it. In a court of law, it would look like Will had gone looking for trouble—especially since Gus was the one walking around with a bullet-torn hand.

Stopping to see Stuart had been just as frustrating.

Will couldn't figure Stuart out. He refused to change his story, still claiming not to know who'd beat him up. It left them no better off, as far as Gus was concerned, than they'd been the night before. Worse, in fact. Because now Gus was more likely than ever to seek revenge, and Will worried that revenge would be aimed at Lindsey. He wanted to shake Stuart. Maybe then he'd see reason. But the younger man was already in bad shape and obviously afraid of something. For the moment, the best Will could do was try to keep Lindsey safe.

If he could get her cooperation.

He waited until they were well out of town and on their way back to the Silver Creek before bringing up the subject.

Bracing himself for the battle ahead, he said, "Lindsey, this thing with Gus isn't over."

"Probably not."

He glanced at her, gauging her reaction. So far, so good. But then, he hadn't gotten to the hard part. "I think we need to take some precautions."

She looked at him, and he sensed her sudden wariness. "What kind of precautions?"

He hesitated, knowing she wasn't going to like what he had to say. "I don't think you should go into town alone for a while."

She turned sideways in the seat. "Really?"

He'd expected the sarcasm, and he pushed on before she could dig her heels in too deep. "Or go anywhere else alone for that matter."

"Give me a break, Will." The sarcasm had given way to disbelief. "You don't really think I'm—"

He cut her off. "Just hear me out."

She sighed loudly and shifted back to face straight ahead. "I'm listening," she said, although her voice said otherwise.

Keeping his eyes on the road, he tried to keep his own impatience in check. "Look, just because Gus and his pal are no longer holed up out at the Schaeffer place, doesn't mean they aren't hiding out somewhere else." There were vacation rentals scattered throughout the foothills. This time of year, many would be occupied, but not all. He threw her a quick glance. "Wherever they are, they're somewhere close."

"I have a ranch to run, Will."

"And who's going to run it if Gus gets his hands on you?"

He heard her sharp intake of breath and pushed on. "Just think about it a minute, Lindsey." He hated scaring her, but if that's what it took to make her use some common sense for a change, he'd do it. "Sooner or later, they're coming after you."

"I'm not going to change my life." He could hear the fear in her voice, along with the defiance, and he hated that he'd caused her either. "I'm not going to let some two-bit hustlers dictate when and where I go."

"Lindsey . . ." He softened his tone, knowing he'd made his point. "It's only—"

"What about you?" she snapped, cutting him off. "Gus isn't too thrilled with you at the moment, either."

"I can take care of myself."

"Hah! Why? Because you're a man?"

"Be reasonable, Lindsey."

"Who got hurt last night? Who's got a two-inch gash in his forehead that should have had stitches?"

"Stop being so damn stubborn for once and think about it. Those two are not going to stop until they hurt you."

That seemed to halt her tirade for a moment, and she turned to stare out the side window. After what seemed an eternity, she said, "Okay, Will, I'll tell you what I'll do. I'll try . . . *try,* that is, to keep a low profile for the next few days."

Will wasn't sure he believed her. "You'll take someone into town with you?"

"Either that, or I'll send someone else instead."

"And on the ranch?"

She hesitated then nodded. "I'll *try.*" Then looking at him she said, "Satisfied?"

No, but it would have to do. "What about putting a watch on your house at night?"

"Don't push your luck."

He smiled and raised a hand in resignation. "Okay."

The house he could take care of himself without her even being aware of it.

"There's one more thing." He paused, looking for the right words and not finding them. So he just said it. "We need to talk about last night." He glanced at her and saw her stiffen.

"I guess there's no getting around it."

"Lindsey, I don't know what happened."

"Don't you? It seemed pretty clear to me."

He laughed briefly. "That's not what I meant. You and I, we've been friends for most of our lives."

"Look, Will, don't worry about it." But there was an edge to her voice. This wasn't any easier for her than him. "Let's pretend last night never happened."

"I can't do that." He hadn't been able to think of much else all morning.

"Then let's just say it was one for the record books. An aberration. We came back after our encounter with Gus, you'd been hurt, things got a little heated—"

"A little heated?" Again, he laughed abruptly. "I guess you could say that."

"Okay, so we got a lot heated." He thought he heard panic in her voice, but decided he must be mistaken. "The point is, this type of thing happens. It was the situation, the—"

Will yanked the truck off the road, threw it in park, and grabbed Lindsey around the waist. Hauling her into his lap, he covered her mouth with his, in a hard kiss that sent his temperature straight through the roof.

At first, she resisted, her hands pressing against his chest. Then suddenly, she seemed to melt against him, responding to his demanding mouth with her own.

When he finally pulled away, her face was flushed, and her eyes held the same heat he'd seen the previous night.

"Just one of those things, Lindsey? Just something that happened?"

"Will . . ."

"Why haven't I been able to put you out of my mind all day? Why can't I forget the way you feel?" He brushed a thumb across her kiss-swollen lips. "The way you taste?"

She shook her head.

"And why, if I pushed you down right here, would you let me make love to you?"

Chapter Nine

Lindsey couldn't answer him. Not with any explanation that made sense. Or one that wouldn't leave her heart exposed and bleeding. Instead, she used her anger as a shield.

Pushing against his chest, she said, "Let go of me."

Will released her, and she scooted to the passenger side of the truck. For a moment, neither spoke, the tension snapping between them like angry wolves.

She considered denying his words, telling him she felt nothing for him. But she couldn't do it. She couldn't lie about something that had become so much a part of her.

"What's the matter, Linds, the truth scare you?"

She flushed, wondering if he'd read her mind. "Who the hell knows the truth? I certainly don't."

"What are you talking about?"

"I'm talking about the fact we've known each other for over twenty years. And in all that time, you've never once expressed any interest in me other than as a friend."

"Things change."

"Yeah, I have something you want." She tossed her

words at him and saw them hit home in the quick flush of annoyance that crossed his features.

"So, we're back to that again."

"You tell me how I can get away from it," she insisted. "How can I believe that you're suddenly interested in me? And that it has nothing to do with the Claxton Ranch."

"Look, Lindsey, whatever *this* is . . ." He hesitated, visibly making an effort to curb his temper. "It has nothing to do with that land. It's between you and me."

"Then explain how it happened. And why now?"

She saw confusion take the punch out of him, out of his certainty. "I can't," he said.

"Well," she lifted her hands, palms up, "there you go."

Just as she'd seen that morning, there was darkness in his eyes, a warning of anger hovering just below the surface. A warning she refused to heed, though she softened her voice. He seemed as baffled by all this as she, and she felt for him. "Look, Will. Maybe you aren't even aware of your own motives. Maybe—"

"That's a load of bull, Lindsey. A load of psychobabble bull. I made love to you last night because I wanted you. I still want you." He turned and threw the truck into gear. "And if you can't deal with that, I suggest you lock your doors tonight. Because I have no intention of staying away from you."

That night, she waited for him.

All day, she'd planned to lock her doors. Riding on anger over his high-handedness, she'd told herself she wouldn't make the same mistake twice. She wouldn't let him into her home, wouldn't give him the opportunity to touch her again and prove his point. She'd given herself one night of memories with Will Claxton. It was enough.

She left the doors unlocked.

Alone in her room, she watched from her window. It was nearly midnight before a lone figure stepped outside the bunkhouse door. He stood for a moment, one more obscure shadow on a moonless night. She sensed him looking her way, searching the house with his eyes until they came to rest on her window. She knew he couldn't possibly see her, but felt certain he knew she was there.

As he started across the empty yard, her heartbeat quickened. She wondered how long it would take to bar the doors against him. Then as quickly as the thought came, it vanished, and she headed for the stairs, flying into his arms as he entered the kitchen.

They never made it upstairs.

She found his mouth, hot and urgent, with no trace of the gentleness he'd shown last night. He backed her up against the kitchen cabinets, wrapped his hands around her waist, and lifted her onto the counter. Pushing her night-shirt above her hips, he stripped off her panties, struggled for a moment with his own clothes, and plunged inside her.

It happened so quick she didn't have time to think, to react or protest. Though she wouldn't have objected. Couldn't. She was ready for him, needing him more than wanting him, and unable to do more than hold on while caught in a maelstrom of sensation strong enough to drown them both.

"Admit it, Lindsey," he demanded, just before his mouth claimed hers with fierce possessiveness. Moments later, or maybe hours, he broke the kiss and his words were a harsh whisper against her lips. "Say you want me."

She moaned, her entire being focused on the sensuous

joining of their bodies, on the turbulence building within her. She couldn't speak, could hardly breathe.

He thrust inside her harder. "Say it."

The crest broke, and tears spilled from her eyes. She tightened her hold on his neck, unable to deny the truth. "I want you." *I love you.*

A moment later, he followed her over the precipice, her name torn from his mouth.

They stayed like that for some time, arms and legs entwined as reality settled back around them.

Slowly, Lindsey became aware of their surroundings.

She heard first the stillness of the dark kitchen and the low hum of the refrigerator. And saw the back door still open wide. She felt the hard, cold counter beneath her, and the warmth of Will's broad shoulders under her hands. He'd taken a shower before coming to her, and she could smell his soap and shampoo, mingled now with the pungent scent of sex. And there was the sharp, hungry taste of him, still lingering on her kiss-swollen lips.

She pulled back to look into his eyes but couldn't speak. There was no need. The last few minutes had spoken more than a thousand words. He'd given her a chance to end this between them before it went further, and she hadn't taken it. She'd given herself over to him, to the passion that she couldn't deny.

At least for now.

Will kissed her again briefly and lifted her off the counter.

"The door," she said, and he took the few steps necessary to kick it closed before carrying her upstairs. Laying her on the bed, he gently removed her nightshirt before shucking his own clothing and lying down next to her. He pulled her into his arms, and she rested her head on his shoulder as he tenderly stroked her hair.

"I may not understand what's between us, Lindsey." His voice was an intimate whisper in the darkness. "Or why now, after all these years. But I know one thing. This is about us." He momentarily tightened his hold on her. "Only us."

Lindsey closed her eyes, holding back the tears that threatened to escape. She wanted desperately to believe him.

* * *

For Will, the next three days seemed unreal.

On the surface, nothing had changed. He helped Lindsey with her ranch while watching for any signs of trouble. Despite her earlier problems, she had a good operation that ran smoothly. Occasionally, the two of them would argue over how a particular chore should be done, but for the most part, they worked well together and the ranch benefited.

Underneath, however, nothing remained the same.

Each night, he went to her and they made love. Sometimes they made hot, frantic love as if they'd never get enough. Sometimes they made slow, tender love as if they had forever. But forever for them was a very short time. Three days. Seventy-two hours. Just until Stuart was released from the hospital.

They didn't talk about it, never actually voiced it aloud, but Will was acutely aware of time running out. It was as if he had a gigantic clock in his head, ticking off the days, the hours, until Lindsey put a stop to their relationship.

He couldn't have said why he knew she planned to end

things between them. Maybe it was the occasional sadness he saw in her eyes after they'd made love, or the way she sometimes seemed to hold back, as if there was some piece of herself she wouldn't share.

On the other hand, he still didn't understand *his* obsession with her. The sex was great, but there was more to it than that. Lindsey had always been his friend, and now she'd become his lover. He needed time, they needed time, to explore and understand this new aspect of their relationship.

Only, Lindsey had no intention of granting them that time. She'd backed away from him again and again, and he'd pushed her, counting on her physical response to give them what little time they'd had. But he couldn't keep on pushing her. At some point, she'd have to decide to continue or end their relationship. Unfortunately, he had a strong feeling which way she'd go.

The morning of Stuart's release came too quickly.

Will lingered longer than usual in Lindsey's bed, unwilling to let their time together end. Lindsey didn't rush him, and he sensed her reluctance as well.

Finally she said, "I promised Stuart I'd be at the hospital by noon."

He knew she expected him to accompany her, but he couldn't. Not this time. He'd pushed her as far as he could. Now it was up to her. "You're going to need to get one of the other hands to go with you."

He saw the surprise in her eyes. And the hurt. "Sure, why not." Grabbing her robe, she climbed from bed.

"I need to take a ride over to the Lazy W," he explained. They both knew it was an excuse. "It's been a week, and I need to make sure everything's running smoothly."

For a moment, she didn't respond, and he watched the

turmoil of emotion behind those green eyes of hers. Silently, he begged her to protest. To demand he go with her. Instead, she said, "Do what you have to."

Her words left him empty in a way he didn't understand. For a moment, he considered changing his mind and pushing her as he'd done before.

He didn't.

Instead, he'd put it all on her. Now it was up to her to decide whether there would be anything else between them. Or not.

* * *

For the rest of the morning, Lindsey fought an overwhelming feeling of disappointment—as if she'd missed something important. She knew it didn't make much sense. Will had obligations, and she certainly didn't need his help to pick up Stuart.

Yet, there was more to it than that.

He'd looked at her so strangely earlier, as if expecting something from her. For a moment, she'd been tempted to confess everything. She'd wanted to tell him how much she needed and wanted him. How much she loved him. Then the temptation had passed, and she hadn't said any of it. Maybe it had something to do with her years of silence, or the fear that his main interest was still the Claxton Ranch. But when it came right down to it, she couldn't even ask him to come with her today.

She couldn't ask him for anything.

One of her crew rode with her to the hospital. It helped that he chattered all the way into town, distracting her somewhat from her thoughts of Will and their strange conversation this morning. After that, there was all the paperwork to fill out for Stuart's release. Before she knew it, they were heading back to the ranch, her brother riding next to her and their hired hand in the back of the truck.

They'd barely cleared the outskirts of town when Stuart asked, "How has Claxton been working out?"

She almost laughed aloud. It seemed she couldn't get away from Will no matter how hard she tried. "It's working out well," she answered. "He's a good foreman, and the men like him." Then, more to herself than Stuart, she added, "Even if he is a bit bullheaded at times."

"I'm surprised you two haven't killed each other."

This time she did laugh. "Oh, it's not that bad. We've had our disagreements. But—"

"It's just that you're so much alike."

Surprised, she glanced at her brother. "Excuse me?"

"Don't tell me you never realized that before."

"I . . . never really thought about it."

Stuart shook his head and let out a short laugh. "You're both about as stubborn as they come. And neither of you will *ever* admit to being wrong. About anything. Plus, you're both too damn proud for your own good. Well . . ." He shrugged. "You get the idea."

Yes, she got the idea. And for several minutes, she didn't say anything. What could she say?

"I don't know if any of that's true," she said finally. Though she suspected he had a point. But what it had to do with anything, she didn't know. "We work well together. Despite our *differences,* things have never run smoother. It's a shame it's only a temporary situation. I could use Will's help—" She glanced at her brother and saw his frown. "What is it?"

"Nothing." He was looking out the side window. "It seems you've done okay without me these last few days."

Her heart went out to him. He would never be the rancher Will was, and they both knew it. But then, Stuart didn't want to spend his life here. Still, she shouldn't have thrown it in his face by going on about Will.

"I missed you," she said, and it was true enough.

He laughed abruptly and shook his head. "So, what's going on between you two?"

Again, he'd surprised her. "What do you mean?"

"Come on, Lindsey. You know what I mean. Have you slept with Claxton yet?"

She felt her face heat. Embarrassment? Irritation? Or both? But she reigned in her emotions and resorted to her standard response when asked about her relationship with Will. "We've always been friends. You know that."

"Cut the bull. You've had the hots for him since you were kids. All anyone has to do is see the way you look at him."

"Stuart, we're—" She almost denied it, but stopped herself. She wouldn't lie about her relationship with Will, but she wouldn't discuss it either. Especially with her brother. "This is none of your business."

He didn't say anything else for a while, and she'd thought he'd let it go. Then he said, "Have you ever questioned why?"

"Why what?" She couldn't hide her irritation.

She glanced over at him, and he rolled his eyes. "Why he's going after you."

"He's not—"

"Lindsey, he wants that land back." Stuart's voice was impatient. "He wants the Claxton Ranch."

To hear someone else voice her own doubts unnerved her. All her defenses went on alert. But who was she defending? Herself? Or Will? "You don't know that."

"Come on, Linds. This is Will Claxton we're talking about. Look at the women he usually spends time with. No offense, but you're not exactly his type."

"Maybe his type has changed."

"Yeah, right."

She couldn't respond to that, couldn't say anything at all at the moment. She was too angry. Only again, she couldn't say at whom.

But Stuart wasn't through. "There's one way to make sure."

She glanced at him.

"Sell him the land. See how long it takes him to run for the hills."

* * *

Will thought he might go crazy.

Stuart had been back at the ranch for over a week, and Will hadn't had more than five minutes alone with Lindsey since.

He realized going to her at night was no longer an option. With Stuart in the house, Lindsey would never allow it. But Will had expected to see her at least, and possibly have some time to talk with her. As it was, he had no doubt she was purposely avoiding him.

He wasn't going to let her get away with it.

If their relationship was over, he wanted to hear her say it. He wanted her to look him in the eye and tell him to take a hike. And he didn't plan to make it easy on her.

He managed to corner her early one morning as she saddled her mare. Coming up behind her, he slipped his arms around her waist. She shied like a startled filly, and he tightened his hold. "Shh, it's only me."

"Will . . ." She clamped her hands around his forearms. "What are you doing?"

Ignoring her protests, he nuzzled her neck. "What does it look like?"

"Please." She managed to pull away and turn to face him. "This isn't the place."

He took a step closer, and she backed up against the side of her horse. He leaned down and nipped at her mouth, gently teasing her. And himself.

When he pulled back, she looked a little less sure of herself. "I agree," he said. "This isn't the place."

"You do?"

Will smiled. "That's why we're going out tonight."

"Out? As in a . . ." She obviously couldn't bring herself to say it.

Will had no such problem. "Date. As in a date."

"But—"

He kissed her, longer this time, until she started to relax, her body melting against his. By then, he knew if he didn't stop soon, he might not stop at all. This time, when he broke away, she looked as breathless as he felt.

"Will—" she started again, but he cut her off.

"Stuart's been home a week, and we've barely had two minutes alone together. If I didn't know better"—he lifted her chin with his fingers—"I'd say you were purposely avoiding me."

The guilt on her face said it all.

"Besides," he continued, not wanting to hear her excuse. "I think we could both use a night away from this place."

She shook her head. "I don't know."

"We'll eat out and then go dancing."

"Dancing?"

"You do know how to dance, don't you, Linds?"

"Of course." She sounded indignant, though Will couldn't ever remember seeing her dance. He couldn't even remember if she'd attended school dances when they were kids. But it didn't matter, he'd teach her.

"Then it's settled," he said.

He could see her uncertainty. She wanted to go—that much was clear. It was the *why* Will couldn't be sure of. She'd never backed down from anything in her life, and if she intended to end their relationship, he was providing the perfect opportunity. On the other hand, there was this physical pull between them, which Lindsey felt as strongly as he. Maybe it was the simple desire to spend time with him that tempted her.

He could only hope.

"Okay," she said finally, and he wondered what had made her decide.

"Good." Releasing her, he stepped back, away from the lure of her. "Be ready at six."

She nodded, and he left the stall.

"Oh, and Lindsey," he said, stopping for a moment and looking back at her. "Wear a dress."

Chapter Ten

The idea of wearing a skirt haunted Lindsey all morning.

Though why she was even considering it escaped her. If Will wanted to take her out, he could do it with her wearing jeans. She wasn't going to pretend to be someone else just so he wouldn't be embarrassed to be seen with her. Besides, she only owned one dress—a simple black shift she'd worn for her father's funeral. She doubted that was what Will had in mind.

Around noon, she headed into town for supplies.

As usual, she wasn't allowed to go alone. Will had enlisted her entire crew in his determination to keep her safe from Gus and his friend. So one of her men insisted on accompanying her. In reality, she could have just sent him on without her, but she didn't.

After loading up at the feed and hardware store, the dress shop across the street caught her eye. She'd only been in it once, to buy the black dress for her father's funeral.

She hesitated.

In truth, she wanted this last evening with Will.

He'd been right. She *had* been avoiding him. Stuart's accusations had echoed in her thoughts for days, and she'd needed time to sort it all out.

In the end, she'd decided that her brother had been wrong. She'd been wrong. She refused to believe that Will would use her to gain possession of the Claxton Ranch. If it turned out she was being naive, so be it. He'd been her friend all her life, and their time together as lovers had been special. She owed him some trust.

No, the problem of continuing a relationship with Will was something else Stuart had pointed out, something less obvious. Something she'd known all along but chose to ignore.

All her life she'd watched Will with other females, bright, pretty girls when they were teenagers, and later, smart, sophisticated women. He'd always had his pick, while Lindsey had hardly created a ripple where men were concerned. Will fell for each and every one of his conquests. For a while. None held his attention more than a few months before he'd grow edgy and bored. Then he would move on.

Lindsey knew he'd never meant to hurt any of those other women, but the area around Willowbend had dozens of broken hearts thanks to Will Claxton. How could she expect to be any different? She didn't even fit his usual type. She was too thin and too tall, with frizzy red hair. She was more likely to challenge a man to a horse race than flirt coyly.

Eventually he *would* grow tired of her, or realize he'd made one big mistake to begin with. Then the situation between them would be awkward—especially because of their lifelong friendship. And though she might not have a choice about losing him as a lover, she wasn't going to lose her best friend again. After all, she'd just found him.

It was time to end things before he broke her heart beyond repair. There was no future for them—she'd understood that from the beginning—and she couldn't go on pretending.

Despite his protests, she sent her hired hand to get some lunch, and she crossed the street. Stopping in front of the store, she glanced around to make sure no one saw her. Then she pushed through the door as a soft bell announced her entrance.

* * *

That evening, Lindsey stood in front of the mirror in her bedroom, wondering about the identity of the woman staring back at her. She looked too feminine, too unfamiliar.

She decided it was her hair.

For once, she'd let it hang loose to frame her face in a riot of red curls. She'd always hated her hair, the color and the way it seemed to have a mind of its own, never behaving or conforming to any manageable style. But tonight it looked . . . different.

Or maybe it was the dress.

After all, she'd never worn anything like it before. When she'd entered the shop in town, she'd planned to pick up a simple denim skirt and top. Instead, she'd ended up buying something completely different. Made of soft, blue floral cotton, the short-sleeved dress fit snugly to her waist, then fell in easy folds to below her knees. A row of small buttons ran from the scooped neckline to the hem, and Lindsey had flushed at the thought of Will taking his time, unfastening each and every one of them.

The dress looked nothing like her, had been far too expensive, and Lindsey had bought it on the spot.

Now she was having second thoughts.

She just didn't look like herself. She thought longingly of her favorite jeans folded neatly in her dresser. She also had that new work shirt she'd bought and hadn't taken out of the plastic wrap yet. So what if the bright red color would clash furiously with her hair? At least she'd feel . . . normal. She started toward the dresser, figuring it would only take her a few minutes to change and braid her hair.

The loud knock at the front door startled her, and her breath caught in her throat. It was too late to change. Or back out.

Calm down, she told herself, *it's only Will.* But in all the years they'd known each other, Will had never knocked at her door. He'd always just walked in. And they'd certainly never gone out on a date. Besides, this wasn't any ordinary date; it would be their first and last as lovers, and she felt like a stranger in her own skin.

She headed down the stairs, her heart beating as if she'd been running. In the front hallway, she paused and once again took a deep breath. Then she opened the door.

Will didn't know what he'd expected, but when he saw Lindsey, he let out a long, slow whistle.

Warm color touched her cheeks. "You're so full of it, Will Claxton."

He stepped through the door, drawn to this new side of her, this softness he hadn't seen before. "Not at all. You look . . ." He took hold of her hands and looked her up and down. Words. He needed words. "Great." *Pretty lame, Claxton.* "Really great." *Oh, that was better.*

Lindsey rolled her eyes and pulled away from him. "Please, I've worn a dress before."

"Not for me, you haven't." He caught her around the waist as she started to move away from him. "Hey, where do you think you're going?" He drew her close, his hands spanning her slim back. "Looking like that, there's no way I'm going to let you get away without a kiss."

"Oh, really?" There was defiance in her words, but her eyes spoke louder. And her voice . . . Lord, the huskiness of it was enough to send him over the edge. "Don't I have anything to say about it?"

"It's totally up to you." He lowered his mouth to within a breath of hers. "Can I kiss you?"

She started to nod, but he couldn't wait.

Claiming her lips, he kissed her deeply, his tongue exploring her mouth while his hands found their own way around the sweet feminine body in his arms. It left him hard and aching.

Not yet, he told himself. *Not here.*

He released her and stepped back, before he could ignore his own resolve to wait. "That's better."

"For whom?" Lindsey swayed on unsteady legs, and he reached out to steady her.

Before he could stop himself, he hauled her back into his arms. He couldn't resist. "Let's try that again."

"You're impossible, Will Claxton." She pushed away from him, but there was laughter in her voice.

"And that's one of my finer qualities." He smiled, unable to resist this woman and the different sides of her that continued to surface and surprise him.

"I think we'd better go," he said. "Or we may not get out of here at all."

"Am I going to be any safer in your truck?"

Grinning, he took her arm and started toward the door. "Probably not."

They drove in silence for several minutes, Will humming with the radio. Lindsey stole an occasional sideways glance at him, obviously trying not to let him catch her.

Telling her to wear a dress had been a last-minute impulse, something that had slipped out before he'd been able to censor his words. He'd never expected her to actually do it. But man, she looked better than any woman had a right to. He didn't particularly like the idea of other men seeing her like that. He would probably have to deck the first cowboy who looked twice—and they *would* look twice. It was a good thing he'd made other plans.

"Where are we going?" she asked, breaking into his thoughts as if she'd read them.

"It's a surprise."

She turned sideways in her seat to look at him. "A surprise?"

He knew that would get her attention. Lindsey never had been able to tolerate surprises. She'd been one of those kids who couldn't even wait for Christmas, searching for her father's hidden stash of gifts whenever he was out of the house.

"You'll just have to wait," Will said, knowing it would drive her nuts.

"But—"

He held up a hand to cut her off. "I'm not going to tell you, Linds. So sit back and relax."

She must have decided he was serious, because she turned back around. "Be that way." If he didn't know her better, he'd have sworn she was pouting.

After a while, they turned off the main road onto a dirt track leading toward the mountains. There was nothing in this direction except open prairie and the river, and he figured it would take her about a second to realize they weren't heading toward town.

She didn't disappoint him. "Will, where *are* we going?"

He threw her a quick smile.

"Is that supposed to be an answer?" Sarcasm laced her voice. "I thought we were going dancing."

"We are."

"What about food? You promised to feed me."

He reached over and snagged her hand, bringing it to his mouth for a quick kiss. "Don't worry. I don't plan to take you home hungry. For anything."

Lindsey snatched her hand back.

The farther they drove, the more he sensed her impatience. Fifteen minutes later, he pulled up beneath a copse of cottonwood trees alongside the Willowbend River. He'd discovered this isolated spot recently, and had thought of Lindsey. The graceful beauty of the trees standing strong against the backdrop of the rugged mountains reminded him of her.

Stopping the truck, he turned in his seat. "What do you think? Better than some overcrowded, smoke-filled bar?"

"It's lovely, but—"

"Don't worry. I'm going to feed you." He motioned toward the back of the truck. "I've got everything we need in the back." Then, reaching across her, he opened the glove box and pulled out a small Bluetooth speaker and his cell phone. "Even the music."

She laughed, and before she could say anything else, he climbed out and circled the truck to open her door. When she hesitated to get out, Will wondered if he'd made a mistake. Maybe she'd been looking forward to going into town.

"If this isn't okay," he said, ready to change his plans

even if it meant keeping an eye on every cowboy they saw, "we can go into town instead."

"No." She shook her head and took his offered hand. "It's perfect."

"Are you sure?"

She smiled again, a soft, feminine smile that warmed her green eyes. "I love it."

He grinned foolishly in relief. He hadn't been wrong. Being gawked at by strangers had never been Lindsey's style. "Come on. I have the perfect spot." He reached into the truck bed and grabbed the quilt he'd brought along.

She looked into the truck as if to carry something. "Let me help."

"Nope." He wrapped an arm around her waist. "Tonight's on me." Despite her protest, he led her over to a large cottonwood and spread the quilt on the grass. "Sit. I'll get the rest."

When she realized her protests would do no good, Lindsey settled on the blanket and watched Will make three trips to bring everything from the truck. First, he brought a large cooler, then two delicious-smelling covered boxes.

"You really are planning on feeding us," she said as he set the last box down.

"Yep, but first . . ." Leaning over, he turned on the portable speaker, then scrolled his phone and made a selection. An old Eric Clapton song, Beautiful Tonight, sweetened the evening air. ". . . we dance." Taking her hand, he pulled her to her feet.

Feeling awkward, she laughed. "Really, Will. This isn't necessary. We don't—"

"Yes, we do. I promised you dancing." He drew her into

his arms and started swaying with the music. "And that's what we're going to do."

Lindsey had never been much of a dancer. As a teenager, she'd been more likely to enter a barrel-racing event at a local rodeo than attend a school dance. But Will made it easy. He held her close, and in his arms, she felt as light as air, drifting with him atop the soft spring grass to Clapton's classic love song.

With a sigh, she rested her head against his shoulder. No wonder he'd broken so many hearts. It was so easy to love him. Too easy.

"What are you thinking?" he whispered against her ear.

"That I missed a lot growing up."

"Like?"

"Dancing." *With you.*

He chuckled softly. "Well, I guess we'll just have to make up for lost time."

She raised her head to look at him, and the warmth in his dark eyes tugged at her heart. At that moment, she could almost believe that he loved her, that he would always love her. And oh, how she wished it were true. She wanted him. Not just now, tonight, but forever. She wanted to dance like this for the rest of their lives. And make love. And wake to see this same softness in his eyes.

Rising on her toes, she kissed him and felt his arms tighten around her. A moment later, she said, "Let's catch up on the dancing later."

Will grinned. He could have danced with her all night, but how could he refuse such a delicious alternative? Lifting her, he carried her the short distance back to the quilt. Together, they stretched out, and he unfastened her top button, stopping to look into her eyes.

"You outdid yourself with this dress, Lindsey."

"You don't like my jeans?"

"Oh, I like them fine." He flipped open another button. "But this is much more fun."

She laughed, and Will quickly took care of another two buttons. Then he stopped. Pushing the dress partially open, he looked at her in surprise.

"Well, well." He ran a finger along the edge of a creamy lace bra. "Now this *is* something new."

"I couldn't wear a plain cotton one with this dress."

"Oh, you could have." He bent his head to brush his lips against the soft skin above the lace, smiling to himself as her nipples visibly beaded beneath the cream-colored silk. "But this is nice too. Real nice."

Sighing softly, she wound her fingers into his hair, holding him close. Will took his time, stroking and teasing the swell of her breasts, though he felt her impatience, her need that was every bit as strong as his.

"What about the rest?" he whispered against her skin. "Any more surprises?"

She groaned, and one by one he unfastened three more of the small buttons, stopping to leisurely kiss her stomach after each one. Finally, he reached her hips and chuckled softly.

"You *do* amaze me, woman." Again, he traced the lace at the edge of her matching panties and followed his caress with his mouth. Lindsey arched against him, and he quickly finished the last of the buttons and pushed the dress aside.

"Don't move." Standing, he quickly rid himself of his unwanted clothing and joined her on the quilt.

For Lindsey, the world became a soft swirl of sensation, of gentle sighs and tender caresses. He teased her and tempted her, bringing her nearly to the brink time after time, before pulling back and starting all over again.

She couldn't say how long their lovemaking lasted. It could have been hours or even days. But when he finally pushed her over the edge, his name spilled from her lips in ecstasy.

Only then did she realize that darkness had fallen.

* * *

Lindsey watched Will sleep.

After making love, he'd retrieved a second blanket from the truck and covered them while they'd polished off the prepared meals he'd brought from one of the restaurants in town. Then they'd lain back down together and made love again, after which Will had fallen into a deep slumber. She, on the other hand, lay next to him, not wanting to close her eyes for even a second.

When he finally awoke, he smiled at her. "Hey, how long have I been out?"

She leaned down and kissed him lightly, her heart breaking. "A while."

"Do that again." He slipped an arm around her waist and tightened his hold.

She did, and a part of her died in the process. When he finally released her mouth, she pulled out of his embrace. It was time.

"Will, we need to talk."

"That sounds serious." He grinned, but it faded quickly.

"It is." Sitting up, she hurriedly put on her underclothes and then her dress, conscious of Will watching her clumsily fasten the buttons he'd so deftly undone. When she finished, she folded her legs against her chest and wrapped her arms around her knees.

"Okay, Lindsey." He slipped on his jeans, an edge in his voice that hadn't been there earlier. "What is it?"

She hesitated, knowing what had to be done and hating it. "We can't go on like this," she said finally. When he started to respond, she interrupted. "Actually, *I* can't go on like this."

"What *exactly* are you referring to?"

He wasn't going to make this easy, and she took a deep breath to strengthen her resolve. "I'm talking about you and me being together as . . ." She couldn't bring herself to say it.

"As lovers?"

"Yes."

"Say it."

She hesitated, but finally forced the words from her mouth. "As lovers. We can't be lovers any longer."

For a moment, he didn't say a word, his gaze fastened on her, and for once she couldn't read what was behind their darkness. "Is this because of Stuart?"

"Well, that's part of it," she hedged. "I can't very well carry on an affair with my brother in the house."

"What's the other part?" Anger crept into his voice, and a hardness into his eyes. "The important part. The part about the Claxton Ranch."

"No." She shook her head and stood, putting distance between them.

Will followed her. "You still believe I'm using you, don't you? That all I want from you is that damn land?"

"No, that's not it." She turned away from him and folded her arms tight around her middle.

"What the hell is it then, Lindsey?" His anger was full-fledged now. "Why are you doing this?"

She spun around. "Because I love you, dammit."

Will went utterly still, and she realized what she'd said.

All those years of keeping her secret, and the words had leaped from her mouth before she could stop them. And there was no taking them back.

"I love you," she said again, gentler this time, resigned to his knowing the truth. "I've always loved you. And I can't . . ." She paused, pressing her lips together to keep back the tears.

He just stood there, staring at her.

"Say something," she demanded.

"I'm stunned. I mean, I never knew. I never thought . . ."

She turned her back on him.

"No, wait, Lindsey." He grabbed her arm and tried to make her turn around. "You surprised me, that's all."

His reaction confirmed what she'd already known, though her heart had hoped she was wrong. He cared about her. Heaven knew the sex was good between them. But love? Well, that was something else entirely.

She started for the truck.

Will came after her, spinning her around and surprising her by pulling her into his arms. "Marry me."

"What?" She pushed away from him with all her strength. "Marry you? Are you crazy?"

"It's perfect. Don't you see?"

"No, I don't see." She was furious. He just didn't get it. She loved him, but she deserved to be loved in return. She didn't want to be just a great bed and ranching partner. "Take me home, Will."

"No, Lindsey, wait. Let's talk about this."

"There's nothing to talk about. Take me home." Before he could say anything else, she climbed into the truck, closing the door firmly behind her.

* * *

Neither of them spoke on the way back to the Silver Creek.

Lindsey sat lost in her pain. She'd handled the whole situation badly. It hadn't occurred to her that she'd hurt Will by calling an end to their relationship. She'd thought she could just say it was over, and things would return to the way they'd always been between them.

What an idiot she was.

Will wasn't ready to end things; he hadn't grown bored with her yet. And the one thing she hadn't wanted to do was lose his friendship, but she'd failed at that as well. How could they remain friends after she'd blurted out her feelings for him?

Although she refused to look at him, she was acutely aware of him in the seat beside her. He sat rigidly and silent, and she could only guess at the thoughts going through his head—some new scheme or plan, no doubt, to make her see things his way.

She shook her head, and thought again how she'd messed up. Their relationship would never be the same.

Then she saw it. The red glow on the horizon.

"Oh my God." She leaned forward. It was every rancher's worst nightmare. "Will . . ."

"I see it."

"Something's on fire." She held a breath a moment. "Near the Silver Creek."

"Hold on." Will floored the accelerator.

Chapter Eleven

I n the yard of the Silver Creek, Will slammed on the brakes, bringing the truck to a screeching halt amid a wake of dust and gravel. Both he and Lindsey jumped from the vehicle almost before it came to a complete stop.

Around them, bedlam ruled.

Men and horses, running, screaming. And the fire, a blazing inferno of noise and heat, raged out of control, sucking life and oxygen from the air.

It only took a moment to assess the situation.

The barn was already lost, though there were men working to save it. They had three heavy-duty hoses directed at the flames, while the rest of the crew had started an old-fashioned bucket chain.

They were wasting their time.

Lindsey grabbed one of the men as he headed toward the well, bucket in hand. "What about the horses?" She had to yell to be heard. "The ones in the barn?"

"All safe." The man barely broke stride, pulling away from her as he raced on.

Will came up behind her. "Lindsey, the house."

She glanced quickly from the barn to the house and nodded. "You're right. The barn's gone."

Together, they shifted the direction of the firefighting efforts. They directed two of the hoses toward the barn side of the house in an attempt to wet it down and keep flying embers and burning debris from catching hold. The third hose they kept on the barn, trying to slow the burning and minimize the risk to the other outbuildings.

At some point, help started arriving, men and women from neighboring ranches undoubtedly answering a phone tree call for help started by one of the hands. Some joined the line alongside Lindsey's men, others set up a first-aid station and carried water to those fighting the blaze.

Will had fought a few fires in his life, but this one burned hotter than any he'd ever seen. It was as if some invisible force fanned the flames, urging them to a feverish pitch. An accelerant, gasoline or some other combustible, was the only explanation he could come up with.

Arson.

A passing thought, and chilling, despite the heat. But it was a thought he couldn't indulge. Not now. Not when the evening breeze threatened to turn stronger, and a shift in direction could send the flames leaping from one building to the next, destroying the entire complex. But their luck held —if you could call such a thing luck—and the wind subsided.

It was hours before they had the blaze under control, and nearly dawn before the last flame flickered and died. Where the barn had once stood, charred fingers of smoldering wood reached toward the slowly lightening sky. Men hovered about exhausted and filthy, unsure what to do next, but afraid to stop lest a stray spark spring to life.

Slowly, the neighbors started to drift off, returning to

their homes, silently thankful, Will knew, that it hadn't been their barn, their ranch, that had burned to the ground. Word of the tragedy would reach the town within the hour, and the entire county would hear of it before noon. Shortly after that, Lindsey would be besieged with food and well-wishers. Whatever good that would do her.

Again, he thought about the intensity of the blaze and knew it hadn't occurred by accident. It wasn't caused by a lightning strike or a faulty electrical circuit. Someone had started this fire and made sure it burned hot.

Will spotted Stuart, arm in a cast, pain etched on his face, and every bit as soot-covered as the rest of them. A week out of the hospital, and he'd fought to save his home as ferociously as any of them.

Approaching the younger man, Will said, "Stuart, go in and get some rest."

He shook his head. "No, I—"

"It's over." Will rested a hand on Stuart's shoulder. "There's nothing more *anyone* can do. Not now, anyway."

Stuart glanced around, seeming to come out of his dazed state a bit. "I guess you're right. Lindsey . . ."

"I'll take care of her."

Stuart nodded, obviously trusting Will with his sister, and started to walk away.

"Stuart," Will said, stopping him.

"Yes?"

"*You* got the horses out." It wasn't a question. One of the men had told Will about it earlier; Stuart had raced into the barn to save the horses even though the fire had already taken hold.

"I spotted the fire first."

"And the men with hoses and the bucket line. You got that organized."

He shrugged. "I should have thought about saving the house. I—"

"You did the right thing. You got things under control."

At first, it looked like Stuart didn't believe him, as if he was waiting for the "but" in Will's words of praise. When it didn't come, a ghost of a smile flickered across the young man's face. "Thanks." Then he turned and headed toward the house.

Next, Will went looking for Lindsey.

He found her sitting on her front porch. The dress she'd worn just for him was filthy and torn. Hell, he'd buy her another, a dozen if she wanted them.

He approached her slowly. "Lindsey?"

She looked up at him, and the streaks of tears marring the soot on her face about killed him. He lowered himself to the porch next to her and wrapped an arm around her shoulders.

A dozen platitudes sprang to his mind, but none were worth speaking. There really was nothing to say in the face of such a disaster. He thought about his arson theory and decided not to mention it. Not just yet, anyway. Sooner or later, he'd tell her. For now, he just sat next to her, holding her.

"I've never seen a fire burn like that," she said, amazing him by so closely echoing his own thoughts. Though why her insight should surprise him after all this time, he couldn't say.

"Me neither."

"Will, the fire was set."

He should have known she'd realize it too. "I know."

Silence fell back around them, and he wondered where her thoughts had taken her. Looking at her profile, at her green eyes brimming with tears, he remembered how she'd looked earlier that evening when he'd first picked her up. She'd been soft and feminine, with light and laughter in her eyes. Later, when they'd made love, passion had transformed her features, and he'd thought he'd never seen a more beautiful woman. A woman in touch with life. Even when they'd argued, her eyes had been alive.

Now, her eyes seemed lifeless, as if she'd given up. "It was Gus," she said flatly. "And his friend."

"That's my theory."

Again, that silence. Only, this time he needed to fill it. He needed to say or do something to bring her back to life.

"It'll be okay," he said, though he knew it was a useless cliché, and she deserved better.

"How is it going to be okay?" she asked, evidently taking him at his word.

"No one was hurt. The horses are all safe. And the house . . ." He glanced behind them. Thank God, they'd been able to keep the house from going up.

"All the equipment in the barn is gone," she countered. "And the barn . . . How will I replace the barn?"

"The insurance—"

She laughed, a sharp hysterical sound that ended in more tears. Pulling away from him, she buried her face in her hands. Will didn't know what to do. He'd comforted enough crying women in his time to know the procedure. But Lindsey was different, and he didn't even know how to begin.

"God, Lindsey. Don't do this." He was afraid to even touch her lest she shatter into a million pieces.

"There is no insurance."

He was too stunned to say anything. You didn't run a ranch without coverage. To do so was—

She didn't let him finish the thought. "They canceled

our policy last month. After twenty-six years, the insurance company decided we'd become too big a risk."

"Because of the accidents?"

She nodded. "I haven't been able to find a new carrier. So you see, for whatever his reasons, Gus succeeded in destroying something that's been in my family for four generations."

For several minutes, neither of them spoke, while Will's mind raced. At the moment, if he could get his hands around Gus's neck, he might just end the man's problems.

"Look, there's a solution to all this," he said. One that didn't include murder.

She looked at him, and he saw the wariness in her eyes.

"I can help you," he said. "I have the cash to rebuild the barn and replace the equipment."

She pulled away from him and stood. "You know I won't accept your charity."

"Not charity." He stood as well and ran a hand through his grimy hair. "A business transaction."

She took a step back. "The Claxton Ranch."

"It's the perfect solution."

She laughed bitterly. "Seems to me I've heard that once already tonight. Only, then you claimed marrying you was the perfect solution."

"Look, Lindsey. I'm just trying to help."

"Yeah, right. You get what you want, Will. Isn't that the bottom line?"

He was too tired for this, too uncertain of everything he felt. All he knew for sure was that this woman meant the world to him, and she needed something he could give. "What is it you want from me, Lindsey?"

"That's the point, isn't it? You haven't the faintest idea."

He stared at her for what seemed an eternity, and then

pushed off the porch. Even knowing she was hurt and scared, he couldn't deal with this now—not without losing his temper and saying a few things he might regret later. He'd made that mistake once before, the night he'd demanded she intervene with her father to save the Claxton Ranch; he wouldn't make the same mistake again. He needed time and distance. Hell, they both needed a little time and distance.

"Well, Lindsey, since you don't seem to need me anymore, I guess I'm finished here."

She lifted her chin a notch. "I guess you are."

For a moment, he didn't move. He wanted . . . No, not now. They would do nothing but hurt each other now.

"If you change your mind about selling that land," he said, "the offer's open. I'll head back to the Lazy W." Then he turned and walked toward his truck.

Halfway there, he stopped and looked back at her. She stood where he'd left her, tall and straight. And too damn stubborn for her own good.

* * *

Even before Will left, Lindsey regretted her words.

He'd been trying to help. Like he'd been helping her for weeks. And tonight, he'd worked alongside her crew, fighting as hard as any man could to save her home. She'd seen him, and marveled at his determination and courage. He deserved better than her sharp tongue and angry accusations.

She considered going after him, but decided against it.

Maybe it was better this way. She'd managed to end their relationship, and, no matter how badly she'd handled things, at least she'd done it. Going to him now would be a mistake. After everything they'd been through tonight, she was too weak and vulnerable. It wouldn't take much, and she'd be back in his arms. Leaning on him. Loving him.

No. It was better to wait. She owed him an apology, and, at some point, she'd probably need to seriously consider his offer to buy the Claxton Ranch. But tonight, she just needed to be alone.

* * *

Over the next few days, Stuart surprised Lindsey by taking charge of the cleanup. It was probably a good thing, because she didn't have the heart for it. Most of the time, she sat in her office, going over the books, trying to figure out how to rebuild the barn and keep the Silver Creek solvent.

Without insurance, she didn't have a whole lot of choices.

She could lay off all her men, and even if she had the heart for such a thing, it wouldn't solve anything. It would leave her with a ranch, but no one to work it. Going to the bank was just as bad, especially considering her run of bad luck.

Which brought her back to Will's offer.

As he'd said, it was a good solution. It would give her the cash she needed to get back on her feet and leave her with a smaller ranch to handle. Not a particularly bad idea at the moment. In truth, her father's acquisition of the Claxton Ranch had left the Silver Creek too large. She'd watched her father struggle with it during his last years.

A knock on her office door interrupted her thoughts.

One of her men stood in the doorway. "I found something you've got to see," he said.

She nodded, and the man crossed to her desk where he

placed something solid folded inside a handkerchief. She slowly peeled back the cloth to reveal an ash-smudged object, its gold stained black from a blazing heat. "Where?" she asked.

"In the barn." He hesitated. "Near where we suspect the fire started."

Stuart's watch.

Chapter Twelve

Lindsey's hand trembled as her fingers touched the scarred surface.

It had belonged to her great-grandfather. He'd brought it west with him from New York, carried it across two thousand miles until he'd found this corner of Wyoming to settle. Since then, it had been passed down from father to son until it belonged to Stuart.

There must be an explanation, some perfectly good reason for the watch being lost. Stuart had told her weeks ago that it was missing. Maybe someone had stolen it. Or he could have pawned it. She wouldn't jump to conclusions as to how it ended up in their barn.

She looked up at the man standing in front of her desk. "Does anyone else know about this?"

"No, ma'am. I thought you should be the first."

"Thank you." She smiled tightly and tried to think. "Okay. Find my brother. Tell him I want to see him."

With a grim nod, the man started to leave.

"And don't mention finding this to anyone else." She closed her fist around the heirloom. "Not even Stuart."

"Yes, ma'am." After he'd gone, the silence descended.

Lindsey didn't move, unwilling or unable. If not for the ticking of the watch, she might have thought time had stopped.

She supposed she should do something while she waited. She could continue looking over the books, go through the day's mail, something. But right now she seemed incapable of any action whatsoever. She should at least plan how best to approach Stuart, how to ask him about the watch. But even that seemed beyond her capacity at the moment. So she sat and waited, the now-cold metal warming beneath her hand.

"You wanted to see me, Lindsey?"

Startled, she looked up at the sound of her brother's voice. He stood in the doorway. She opened her mouth to say something, but no words escaped. Instead, she picked up the watch, turned it in her palm, and held it out to him.

Stuart crossed the room, obviously puzzled, but when he saw the watch, guilt flashed across his features. It was all the answer she needed, and she felt his betrayal go through her like an icy wind.

For several seconds, neither of them spoke. Finally, Stuart said, "Where did you find it?"

"One of the men found it in the barn." Tears stung her eyes, but she forced them back. "In the ashes."

Stuart sighed and turned to walk to the windows. With his back to her, he said, "What are you going to do?"

"Why don't you tell me how it got there?"

"But you already know." He shrugged. "At least you think you do."

"Did you start the fire?" She could hardly get the words past the obstruction in her throat.

He swung back around to face her, his eyes hot with anger. "No!" Then he shook his head, a sudden note of resignation shadowing his voice. "I swear, I had nothing to do with the fire."

Lindsey closed her eyes briefly, thankful for this one small reprieve.

Stuart moved back across the room and sank into a chair as if unable to hold himself erect any longer. "You may not believe this, but I tried to stop them."

"Them?" Though she knew who he meant.

He hesitated a moment, running a hand through his hair. "Gus and Ray."

"I see."

"No, you don't *see* anything." With renewed energy, he leaned forward. "I never wanted it to go this far. Never expected . . ." He stood again, seething with frustration. "Oh, what's the point? You're not going to believe me." Shoving his hands into the pockets of his jeans, he crossed back to the windows. "So why don't you just call the sheriff and get it over with?"

"I'm not calling anybody." She tried to keep her own voice calm, though inside she reeled. "At least, not until I know what happened."

After a moment, he said, "Look, I've never made it a secret that I want off this ranch." He paused, as if gathering his thoughts. Or the words to express them. "While Dad was alive, I stuck around because . . ." He shrugged, a slow lift and fall of his shoulders. "Well, I thought he might need me."

He faced her, and she again saw his anger. Only, this time, it wasn't directed at her. "Of course, he never did. Why would he? He had you." His voice broke, but he pushed on. "I just never expected him to tie me to this place forever."

"You could have left."

He let out an abrupt laugh. "Sure. With what? Dad made sure I was stuck here forever. Either I became a rancher, or I became nothing."

"So you decided to destroy everything? You. Me. The ranch."

"No. If you hadn't made that damn promise . . ." He threw out a hand in a sweeping gesture, and then dropped it limply to his side. "I thought if I could put enough stress on you, you'd be forced to sell off part of the ranch. Will Claxton is champing at the bit to get his hands on that land. If you sold it to him, you could buy me out and I'd be free. Everyone would win."

"You caused the accidents." Again, it wasn't a question.

"Only a few." He slipped his hands back into his pockets and looked away. "I hired Gus to cut the fences and interrupt the feed supply."

"How did you pay him?"

He shrugged again. "I had a little cash put away. Enough for a down payment. I promised the rest once I got my part of the inheritance. Once you sold to Claxton." Another flash of guilt crossed his features. "But you dug in your heels and things got out of hand."

"Someone could have been hurt, Stuart. Or killed." Disbelief echoed in her voice. *"You* were almost killed."

"I never expected Gus to take things into his own hands."

Lindsey couldn't believe her brother could be so naive, trying to control a man like Gus. Yet she hurt for Stuart too. Their father had never been an easy parent, and he'd been harder on his son than his daughter. But then, Lindsey had

144

taken to ranching as easily as breathing, and Stuart had fought it every step of the way. Possibly, if her father had let Stuart go his own way, he'd be a different man now. But she couldn't blame her father for Stuart's actions. He was a grown man.

"You've got to believe me, Lindsey. I never meant to hurt anyone. The rock slide was Gus's idea. I didn't even know about it until after. He was just supposed to rustle a few head of cattle, but after our run-in at the Spur, he went a little crazy."

"But you knew Gus was responsible." She tried to keep the anger out of her voice. "You *told* him the location of the herd and where to ambush them."

"I tried to call the whole thing off. But things had gone too far. He wanted more money. That's when—"

"They beat you up."

"Gus agreed to call it off only if I could pay him. I gave him the watch as collateral. But he wanted cash." He paused and pressed his lips together. "He wanted ten thousand dollars."

Lindsey just stared at him, having no idea how to react to all he was telling her. Her automatic response was anger, but she knew that wouldn't do either of them any good.

"Of course," Stuart continued, "I didn't have anywhere near that amount."

"Why didn't you come to me? We could have gone to the sheriff together."

"I thought I could handle it myself."

Again, Lindsey shook her head. "And the fire?"

"I hadn't been sleeping too well and went downstairs for a drink. I saw movement near the barn, but by the time I got down there, Gus and Ray were taking off. I tried to stop them." He turned back to the windows. "But it was too late."

"What about the watch?"

"They must have planted it, trying to make it look like I'd started the fire." Again, he paused. "And it worked."

For several long minutes, neither of them spoke. Lindsey sat watching her brother's rigid back, her mind racing while her heart broke for him. He'd never grown up, never learned to take responsibility for his actions.

Maybe this was his chance.

"Will you go to the sheriff now?" she asked.

Stuart turned and looked at her without answering.

She repeated her question. "Will you testify against Gus and Ray?"

He visibly took a deep breath. "I don't want anyone else hurt."

Lindsey smiled tightly, relieved. It was a first step. "Okay, then. We'll go into town today."

Stuart shook his head. "This is my doing, I'll go alone."

Lindsey rose and circled the desk to him. "No matter what you did, we're family. I'll stand by you."

For a moment, he didn't look like he believed her. "I haven't been much of a brother to you."

"I'm not sure Dad or I ever gave you much of a chance." She reached over and picked up their great-grandfather's watch. "You forgot something."

Stuart looked from her to the watch and back again. "I think you should keep it."

"No, it's yours."

With a grim smile, he accepted the watch. "I'm sorry, Lindsey. I tried, but I'm just not as strong as you."

Strong was the last thing she felt right now. "That's not true, Stuart. You're just not a rancher."

Stuart put his arms around her, and Lindsey felt the tears slip down her face. She couldn't remember the last time her brother had hugged her.

* * *

Straightening things out with the sheriff took most of the day. He wasn't as forgiving as Lindsey, but then, Stuart wasn't his brother. In the end, arrest warrants were issued for Gus and Ray, and Stuart faced charges of conspiracy and obstruction of justice. In addition, the sheriff suggested Stuart remain in town, courtesy of the jail, until the other two men were in custody. Just to be on the safe side.

So it was after dark by the time Lindsey returned to the Silver Creek. The smell of burned wood permeated the air and made her think longingly of Will. For weeks, she'd had him to talk with and confide in. Although she'd been loath to admit it, he'd helped carry her burdens and lightened her load. Now she was all alone again.

Suddenly, she had to see him.

She came up with several good reasons, all of which made perfect sense. She owed him an apology, and she wanted him to hear about Stuart's arrest from her instead of the local rumor mill. Plus, she had an offer to make him concerning the Claxton Ranch. Of course, those were all just excuses.

The truth was, she missed him terribly and nothing seemed as important right now as seeing his face, his smile. And hearing his voice.

* * *

Will couldn't sleep.

Hell, he hadn't gotten any sleep since the night of the fire. Every time he closed his eyes, he saw Lindsey. Thinking about her was a constant thing, eyes open or closed.

He sat with his feet propped on the railing of the wide porch that wrapped around three sides of the Lazy W's main house. Next to him on the table sat a tumbler of Scotch. Untouched.

He loved her. It was as simple and as complicated as that.

He'd thought about heading over to the Silver Creek at least a dozen times a day to tell her, but he doubted whether she'd believe him. Not now anyway. Especially after the absolutely brilliant way he'd handled *her* declaration.

Lindsey loved him.

He still couldn't believe it. And at the time she'd said it, he'd been stunned to the point of stupidity. He'd never considered love before. The word hadn't been in his vocabulary. But the more he'd thought about it these past few days, the more he realized that was exactly what he felt for Lindsey. Why she drove him nuts, day and night. And why no other woman had ever managed to keep his attention for more than a few months. Lindsey had always been there, eclipsing every other female in sight.

Of course, if he told her that, she'd probably laugh in his face.

He needed to give her time to calm down and do some thinking of her own. Eventually he'd go to her and make her understand. She had to realize they belonged together.

It was close to midnight when he heard the approaching vehicle. Dropping his feet to the floor, he waited until he recognized Lindsey's truck. Surprised, he stood, and as she climbed out, he moved to the top of the steps. She crossed the yard and stopped. In the darkness, he couldn't see her expression, but he sensed her uneasiness.

"You're out late, Lindsey," he said as he crossed his arms and leaned against the railing. "Doesn't seem too safe."

"I have to talk to you."

His heart gave a jolt, but he steadied himself. She could be here for any number of reasons that had nothing to do with the two of them and what they'd shared.

"Come on in, then." He kept his voice steady, though he felt nothing of the kind. Turning, he headed back inside and she followed. "Have you ever been to the Lazy W before?" he asked, resorting to small talk.

"No." She shook her head. "It's—"

"It's not your typical ranch." He led her into a large great room. "The owner's never lived here. He just comes out from Denver occasionally to check up on things."

She looked around, moving to the center of the room and turning to take in the cedar paneling and beamed ceiling. She was stalling, and they both knew it. Now that Will could see her face clearly, he saw her agitation.

"What did you want to talk about, Lindsey?"

Finally, she faced him, but didn't speak. He understood. There was so much they needed to talk about. Where did either of them start? Finally, she said, "I came to see if you're still interested in buying the Claxton Ranch."

Her statement took him aback, though he'd known it would eventually come to this. Lindsey was stubborn, not stupid. Still, he hadn't expected her to drive all the way over here in the middle of the night to tell him she'd changed her mind about selling off a part of her ranch.

Something had happened.

He crossed the room to the bar. It was his turn to stall. "Would you like a drink?"

"No." She folded her arms as if to plant herself firmly in the middle of the room. "Are you still interested in the Claxton Ranch or not?"

In all honesty, he no longer had an answer for her. A month ago, he would have jumped at the opportunity. He'd thought he wanted nothing more than to run his own ranch, riding his own range and working his own herd. Now it no longer seemed so important. Not that he didn't still want those things, but something else, *someone* else, meant more to him. And she stood before him, expecting him to jump at the opportunity to buy back his family's land.

Setting down the bottle he'd been about to open, he leaned against the bar. "What happened, Lindsey?"

"What makes you think something happened?" She tried to sound casual, nonchalant, but the underlying nervousness in her voice betrayed her.

He laughed briefly. "Three days ago, you kicked me off your place for making you an offer on that land."

She looked distinctly uncomfortable, unfolding her arms and slipping her hands into the back pockets of her jeans. "I didn't exactly kick you off the ranch."

He just continued to look at her, knowing eventually she'd spit it out.

"Okay," she said, pulling one of her hands free to swipe at the stray curls that had escaped her braid. "I apologize for the other night. I was wrong."

"Yes, you were." He paused, letting his words sink in before adding, "But . . . it had been a rough night. All of it."

She blushed and looked away, obviously remembering the hours before the fire, just as he was.

"Now," Will said, drawing her back to the present and her reason for showing up on his doorstep at midnight. "I want to know what happened to change your mind about selling me that land."

She moved away from the center of the room to a row of bookshelves that lined one wall. Picking up a small hand-carved wooden statue, she examined it before returning it to its spot. "I started looking over my finances—"

"The truth, Lindsey."

She glanced at him, a flash of anger in her green eyes.

"Oh, I don't doubt you need the money, but I know you too well to believe that's all there is to it."

She hesitated a moment longer, then seemed to fold into herself as she sank onto one of the nearby couches. "Okay, it's Stuart. I want to buy him out."

That surprised him. "I thought you'd promised your father not to sell."

"I did." She took a deep breath. "But he was wrong to ask for that promise. And I was wrong to agree."

He couldn't keep his distance any longer. Crossing the room, he sat next to her and took her hand. She didn't resist.

"Tell me," he said.

She hesitated a moment then sighed. "Stuart started the accidents." She leaned back against the couch and closed her eyes. "He hired Gus to cut our fences and steal the feed shipments. And then . . . things got out of hand."

Will listened as she explained about Stuart and Gus's arrangement and how it had led to the fire. Then she told him about Stuart's arrest. At some point, she moved away from the couch, pacing the floor like a caged wildcat.

Will hurt for her. Even though Stuart and Lindsey had never been close, Will knew how much she loved her brother—and to have him betray her . . . Will wanted to shake the younger man.

When she finished her story, she stood facing him once again, arms crossed, her eyes hot and dry. "That's it."

"I'm sorry, Lindsey."

She brushed his words aside with a wave of her hand. "At least Stuart finally told the truth. And now he's going to have to face the consequences."

He wanted to go to her, but suspected she wouldn't welcome his touch right now.

"So," she said. "That brings us back to why I want to sell off part of the ranch." She hesitated, and he suspected this wasn't easy for her. "When this is all over, I want to buy Stuart out. I want to give him a chance to make something of himself."

Will sighed and pushed himself off the couch, heading back to the bar. That drink he'd started to fix earlier sounded really good.

"Why do I get the distinct feeling you're avoiding answering me?" she asked.

He poured two fingers of Scotch, paused, and then added another inch of the dark liquor to the glass. "I have to think about this, Lindsey."

"I see." There was a touch of irritation in her voice. "I thought you'd said the offer was open."

"Things have changed." Like the fact that what he wanted *now* was Lindsey, no strings attached and nothing between them. Not the land and not her brother. And if he bought the Claxton Ranch from her, she'd never be sure if he loved her or was just grateful for once again having control of his family's land. "I need a little time."

She crossed her arms, her gaze locking on his. "How much time?"

He shook his head. "I'm not sure. A couple of days, maybe."

For a moment, she didn't say anything. "Okay. I'll give you two days. After that, I'm going to make it general knowledge that the land is up for sale."

Will nodded. "Fair enough."

"Well . . ." She unfolded her arms and glanced around. "I guess I'd better get going."

"It's probably a good idea." If she didn't leave soon, he wasn't sure he'd let her out the door. "I'll follow you."

"There's no need." She started toward the door. "I know my way."

"I'm sure you do." He came up beside her and slipped an arm around her shoulder. It probably wasn't a good idea to touch her, but the alternative was unthinkable. "But Gus and Ray are still out there."

She started to object, and he pressed a finger to her lips before lowering his head for one brief kiss. It was all he dared allow himself. "Don't argue with me."

For once, she didn't.

* * *

Lindsey stood at her front window and watched the taillights of Will's truck disappear. He'd followed her all the way back to the Silver Creek and waited until she was inside before leaving. But he didn't kiss her again, didn't touch her, didn't even get out of his truck. It was probably for the best. As it was, all the way home, she'd been unable to think of anything but that one brief touch of his lips.

It had taken all her remaining energy, all her courage, to go to him tonight. To apologize and offer him the Claxton Ranch. She'd expected him to snap it up. He hadn't, and that puzzled her. But she was too tired, too mixed up to think about anything more tonight.

Letting the curtain drop, she turned toward the front hallway. Halfway across the room, a large hand clamped down on her mouth.

"Well, well," said a sickeningly familiar voice as she felt a gun rammed against her side. "If it isn't the little ball-breaker herself."

Chapter Thirteen

Lindsey froze.

The gun at her side—cold, hard, and deadly—was the only thing real about this situation.

"I'm going to move my hand," Gus said. "If you scream, it will be your last."

She nodded, and he shifted his hand to her upper arm. "What do you want?"

"Oh . . . I think you know what I want."

Lindsey fought a wave of nausea. "Money? Is that it?" She tried to still the trembling in her voice but failed. "I can get—"

"Too late. Things have gone too far for that now. Don't ya think, Ray?"

"You bet." The second man stepped up beside them, waving a length of rope in her face.

"You won't get away with this," she said. "There are twenty cowboys on this ranch. All I have to do is scream and—"

"Yeah." Gus pressed closer, his breath hot and foul against her cheek. "And I figure five of 'em will be dead before they know what hit them. So, for their sake, let's hope you know how to keep your mouth shut.

"Tie her up." He stepped in front of her, the gun now visible as Ray grabbed her arms and yanked them back. "But don't worry, we'll get our money and the rest of what's comin' to us.

"Make sure you get those knots real tight," he said. "We don't want to lose our prize."

Lindsey fought her rising panic. "You'll never get away with this."

"Maybe not. But you're gonna learn some manners." He ran the gun's muzzle down her chest, stopping at the vee of her blouse. "I'm gonna teach you what it means to cross old Gus."

"There's a warrant out for your arrest." She tried not to think about the gun, or the threat behind Gus's words. "The sheriff and his men are looking for you right now."

"Just another reason to bring you along."

"Look, I have some cash in the house. It's yours. Take it and head up into the hills. With any luck, you'll get away."

"Don't need luck. We got you."

"If you do this, they'll never stop looking for you."

"I'm counting on it. Especially that cowboy hero of yours. I can't wait until he comes for you."

"You'll—"

"Gag her. I've had just about all I can take of her whining."

"No—"

Ray crammed a rag in her mouth before she could voice another useless objection and tied a bandanna around her head to keep it in place.

"Now, the three of us are gonna walk out to your truck," Gus said. "All natural like. Be smart. We don't want to attract any attention. Got it?" When she didn't respond, he pressed in closer. "Got it?"

This time, she nodded and he ushered her through the door, holding her snug against his side while pressing the gun into the small of her back. "Easy now," he said. "I sure would hate to pull this here trigger before I get a sample of the goods."

He stopped next to her truck, and Ray squatted down to tie her feet before lifting her and dropping her into the bed of the truck. She fell with a thud that sent shocks of pain shooting through her arms and legs.

"Careful," Gus said with a short, nasty laugh. "We don't want to bruise all that soft white flesh." Again, he poked the gun at the top of her breast. "Not till we've had our fill anyway."

Lindsey squeezed her eyes shut.

Gus laughed again. "One more thing . . ."

Lindsey reopened her eyes, fresh terror washing through her as he leaned into the truck bed, a knife in his hand now instead of the gun. Grabbing her by the hair, he roughly sawed off a piece.

"Need a calling card," he said, holding up the ragged curl for her to see.

He patted her cheek and then the two men moved off.

She fought the tears as she listened to them climb into the truck's cab and start the engine. She'd fallen into a nightmare. Only, somehow, she knew she wasn't going to wake up.

* * *

Will snapped awake.

He'd finally gotten to sleep, for the first time in what

seemed like days, and now someone was banging on his back door. He glanced at the bedside clock. Four a.m. With a curse, he threw back the covers and headed downstairs.

"I'm coming," he yelled as the pounding continued.

In the kitchen, he switched on the porch light. After glancing outside, he yanked the door open. "What the hell are you doing here?"

Eric stepped inside. "We got problems."

"This better be good . . ."

"I found this note nailed to my door when I got home tonight." He handed a piece of paper to Will. "It's from Gus. He's got Lindsey."

Icy fear slithered down Will's spine.

Forcing himself to take the note, he read quickly. It was brief and explicit. Gus and Ray were holding Lindsey in an old cabin up in the foothills. They wanted supplies for two weeks, three horses, and ten thousand dollars in cash. Will was to come alone. Otherwise, he'd never see Lindsey alive again.

Taped to the page was a single red curl. Lindsey's.

Will crushed the note as white-hot rage engulfed him. "That son of a—"

"Take it easy, man," Eric said. "I know you want to go charging out there like some kind of commando, but you need to think this through."

"Like hell." Grabbing a saddlebag from the mudroom, Will started toward his office.

Eric followed. "Think about what you're doing."

"I am thinking." Just the thought of Gus's hands on Lindsey sent ribbons of fury slicing through him. He tossed the bag on his desk and went for the gun rack. After pulling down a Winchester, he grabbed a box of .30-06 cartridges from the drawer beneath the cabinet. "I'm going to get Lindsey back alive."

"This isn't the way to do it."

Will carried the rifle and ammunition to his desk. "You got a better idea?"

"Yeah, let the sheriff handle it."

"Feel free to call him." Opening the desk drawer, Will took out the Colt he kept for emergencies. "But it'll take him an hour to get here from town"—he loaded the revolver —"and another hour or more to get up to that cabin." Slapping the cylinder closed, he slipped the .45 into his belt. "Meanwhile, I'm heading cross-country on horseback, it's faster and Gus won't be expecting it. By the time the sheriff arrives, I'll have Lindsey back."

"Or you'll both be dead."

Will stopped and faced the other man. "I'm not leaving her in that man's hands for one second longer than necessary."

"And if he kills you first? What good will you be to her then?"

He'd thought about that—for about two seconds. "It's a risk I've got to take."

"You're not thinking straight."

Will ignored him. Shoving his desk chair aside, he tossed back the small throw rug covering the floor safe, squatted down to work the combination, and then opened the heavy iron lid.

Inside was his bargaining power.

"Damn," Eric said from behind him. "Who the hell knew you had that kind of cash?"

Will emptied the safe, tossing the bundles on top the desk. "Wouldn't have been too hard to figure out." Dropping the door back in place, he spun the lock. "My men get paid every other Friday. And they like cash." Standing, he shoved the money into the saddlebag.

"You don't really think Gus is just going to hand her over?" Eric moved closer. "With or without that money? This is a trap."

Will looked up and slung the bag over his shoulder. "That's what this is for." He reached for the Winchester.

Eric grabbed the rifle first.

Will glared at the other man. "Don't get in my way, bartender."

"If you insist on being a damn fool, I'm going with you."

"Give me that gun."

Eric rested the rifle across his shoulder. "This thing's not going to do you a damn bit of good. Not close up, anyway. We'll have one of your men call the sheriff, but I'm coming with you."

"You can't ride worth a damn. You'll slow me down."

"But I'm a hell of a shot. Tie me to the saddle if necessary but get me out there. I'll cover you from the trees. Make sure Gus keeps his part of the bargain."

Will hesitated, gauging the other man, and then nodded. After all, Lindsey's life was at stake, and he could use all the help he could get. Besides, Eric had been a Marine Scout Sniper and his skill was legendary even within that elite group. "Let's go."

* * *

Lindsey hurt.

Blindfolded and lying tied hand and foot, her arms and legs ached from the constant jarring against the unyielding metal of the truck bed. She couldn't steady herself or limit the punishment to her body. The only thing she could do was try to keep her head up. Mostly, she failed even in that, and her head pounded with an intensity that brought tears to her eyes with each new jolt.

She had no idea how long they drove or which direction they were headed. They'd stopped once, early on, and she'd had a brief hope that they were still fairly close to the ranch, but then the truck started moving again. After that, it seemed like forever, her entire life coming down to this hard, cold trip. But despite the pain, she didn't want the truck to stop again as they drove farther away from any possible help. More than anything, she feared reaching their destination.

She thought of Will, all the things they'd said to each other, and the things they hadn't. *I love you,* she said over and over again in her mind, wishing she'd told him in some other way instead of blurting it out as she'd done the night of the fire. Now it was too late.

Pulling her thoughts back to the moment, she tried to devise a plan, but fear numbed her mind. She pushed it down, focusing instead on her options. Only, there didn't appear to be very many. If she could somehow break free and make a run for it, she might get away. She knew these mountains and would willingly take her chances against the elements rather than face Gus and Ray. It seemed like a workable plan.

Except for her bound legs. And the gun.

When the truck finally came to a jarring stop, the sudden silence nearly deafened her. As from a distance, she heard the doors open and slam shut, and she clamped her eyes closed.

When she opened them, Gus stood over her, grinning. "Time for your lesson." He grabbed her arm, and panic seized her. Shaking her head violently, she jerked away from him. He laughed, a low sound that made her skin crawl.

Ray appeared next to him. "She sure do got spunk."

"I like my women wild. Makes 'em more fun to tame." Again that laugh, and bile rose in Lindsey's throat.

She had to get away.

"How long before her boyfriend shows up?" Ray asked.

Lindsey went still at the mention of Will. They'd kill him, and that frightened her more than anything.

"I bet she's wondering the same thing." Gus slid the gun from his waistband and waved it in her direction. "Depends on how long it takes that bartender to pass on our note. But, I figure we got at least a couple of hours, probably more."

Lindsey's mind raced, trying to outrun the fear that threatened to overwhelm her. These men were going to kill her. Kill Will. And there didn't seem to be anything she could do to stop them.

"But he'll be here," Gus said, turning to Lindsey. "Of course, it'll be too late for you by then."

Lindsey's fear faded to anger. Sharp, hot, mind-clearing anger. They were using her as bait, and she couldn't let them get away with it. Somehow—

"Get her out of there and bring her inside," Gus said as he moved away from the truck.

She fought, squirming and kicking as Ray tried to get hold of her arm. There was no gun now, and no one else to get hurt. They were planning to kill her anyway. And Will. But she wasn't going to go down without a fight.

After a few minutes of trying to lift her over the side of the truck, Ray dropped the tailgate with a curse and climbed in. Kneeling next to her, he gripped her hair and yanked her to a sitting position.

Tears of rage and pain blurred her eyes.

"Either you're gonna get out of this here truck without any more trouble," Ray said, "or I drag you. Understand?"

She nodded. She understood all too well.

He climbed out of the truck, hauling her with him. When he set her on her feet, she swayed as if her legs were too weak to hold her, hoping he'd untie her feet. Instead, he bent down and hoisted her over his shoulder. Rubbing her bottom, he said, "That's more like it."

It was all Lindsey could do not to choke.

Inside the cabin, he set her down, and Gus pulled the gag from her mouth. "Now it's time to learn those manners."

She took a deep cleansing breath and spat in his face.

"Why you . . ." Gus backhanded her, knocking her to the floor. "Do that again, bitch,"—he pointed an accusing finger at her—"and I'll make sure no one ever looks twice at that face of yours again."

"Come near me again," she snarled, "and I'll use my teeth."

Ray laughed but stifled it instantly as Gus shot him a murderous glance. "Untie her feet."

"Yeah, Ray," Lindsey said, stretching out her legs. "Come untie my feet."

Ray glanced nervously at Gus. "I'm not too—"

"Untie her feet."

Ray squatted, and Lindsey kept perfectly still, waiting. He held her legs as he cut the knots, but they both knew what was coming. The rope fell away, and she remained motionless a moment longer, until he relaxed a fraction. Then she kicked out, catching him on the side of the head.

Ray howled and backed up, cradling his ear with his hand. He pulled a gun from his belt and pointed it at her. "Let's just kill her now and get it over with."

Lindsey stared at the gun and froze. She didn't want to die, but better to go with one quick bullet than to let these two put their hands on her. Besides, she didn't believe they'd kill her yet. Not until Will arrived and they had everything they wanted.

Gathering her courage, she smiled tauntingly. "Go ahead, Ray, pull the trigger."

Ray's face reddened. "Why you—"

Gus knocked Ray's gun hand skyward as he squeezed the trigger. "You moron, that's exactly what she wants you to do."

Ray backed up, cursing, and then turned toward the window at the sound of horses outside. "Gus, someone's here. You said it would be a couple of hours."

"Cross-country," Lindsey taunted. "Guess you two geniuses didn't figure on how much quicker that would be."

* * *

Will reined in his Appaloosa at the base of an old gravel road heading off toward the hills. They'd been riding hard for over an hour, loaded down with the extra horses and supplies, and both the men and animals were beginning to feel it.

Eric edged up beside him. "This it?"

Will nodded. "This is as far as you go. The cabin's about a quarter mile up that road."

"Thank God." Eric slid to the ground with a groan. "I may never walk normally again."

"I'd worry about that *if* you live through the day."

"Yeah." Eric slid the Winchester from its scabbard. "You've got a point."

"I'll give you a five-minute head start." Will glanced at his watch. "Follow the road but keep under cover."

"You got it." Eric handed over his horse and nodded. "Good luck."

"You too."

Eric jogged toward the trees, disappearing beneath the canopy of ponderosa pine. Will waited the time they'd agreed, and then nudged his horse toward the road. He took it slow, leading the three extra animals, watching and listening for anything that didn't belong in these woods.

Then he heard the shot.

He reacted before he could think, urging his mount forward and taking the road at a full gallop. Within seconds, the woods gave way to a clearing surrounding a small run-down cabin, and he reined back, bringing all four horses to a chaotic stop.

Scanning the area—the cabin, Lindsey's truck, the surrounding trees—he heard nothing. Just the silence of the hills, the snorting and pawing of the animals, and his own heartbeat.

"You made pretty good time, cowboy."

The hateful voice shattered the silence, and Will steadied his horse while going for the Colt at his waist.

"I wouldn't do that." Gus emerged from the cabin, holding a gun to Lindsey's head. "Unless you want to see her lose more than a few hours' sleep."

Will sought Lindsey's eyes, seeing in them everything he loved about this woman. Her anger and determination. Her stubborn pride. Her courage.

He was going to get her out of this.

She seemed to read his mind, because she nodded almost imperceptibly.

"Okay, Gus." Will raised his hand away from the gun.

"I'm here and I brought everything you asked for." He dropped the lead rope for the three riderless horses and backed the Appaloosa a couple of steps.

"Get them," Gus said to Ray.

Ray moved cautiously forward and grabbed the rope.

"You got a two-week supply of food and water there," Will said, as Ray quickly examined the saddlebags. "Take it and go."

"I don't see no money," Ray said.

"Where is it, cowboy?"

"I got it." Will rested his hand on the saddlebags in front of him. "Right here."

"Throw it down."

Will shook his head. "Let her go first."

"What if I just shoot her instead?" Gus pressed the gun hard against her head, and Lindsey flinched.

"Okay . . ." Will reached down and unfastened the bag. "You win." As he tossed it on the ground, he prayed Eric was as good a shot as he claimed, and that he was out there somewhere with his sights set on Gus.

Retrieving the bag, Ray opened the flap and grinned. "It's here."

"Okay, cowboy, get down." Gus waved the gun at Will.

Will hesitated, knowing he'd lose any minor advantage by dismounting. In the end, he had no choice. Gus now held all the cards.

Once Will was on the ground, Ray took the Appaloosa's bridle and led the animal over to Gus.

"Now we're gonna take us a little ride," Gus said, shoving Lindsey toward the horse.

"That wasn't the deal," Will said, though he'd known Gus would try this. "You got your money. Now let her go."

"You didn't really think we were gonna just forget the

way you did us? You *owe* us, cowboy. And we always collect our debts. Besides"—Gus waved the gun at Lindsey—"we ain't had our fill yet."

Rage surged through him at Gus's insinuation, but Will tamped it down. It wouldn't help, and it could get them both killed. For Lindsey's sake, he needed to remain calm— no matter how much he wanted to ram that gun down Gus's throat.

Ray took hold of one of the Appaloosa's stirrups and held it out for her. "Put your foot in."

"How do you expect me to mount with my hands tied behind my back?" Lindsey asked.

"Do it."

Lindsey glared at Gus but complied, lifting her foot awkwardly into the stirrup. As Ray boosted her up, she threw a quick glance at Will, and he saw their chance. And Gus's mistake.

Lindsey struggled into the saddle, clumsily shifting in an attempt to gain her balance. With a curse, Ray steadied her and straightened the stirrups. Will saw it coming. Lindsey righted herself, looked Ray square in the eye, and struck out with one booted foot, catching him in the jaw and sending him sprawling.

Will leaped forward, hoping she'd had time to regain her balance, and smacked the Appaloosa on the rump, sending him running toward the trees.

Gus hollered and raised his gun, but the crack of rifle fire and the smack of a bullet near his feet brought him around to face the woods. Will dove for him.

They went down in a cloud of dust and flying limbs, all of Will's rage surging to the surface. It was over quickly, much quicker than the last time he'd wrestled with Gus. Maybe it was adrenaline or residual fear for Lindsey, but the next thing Will knew, Eric was pulling him off the nearly unconscious man.

"That's enough," Eric said. "You're going to kill him."

Will backed up, his hands trembling as he realized how close he'd come to choking the life out of the other man. Then his thoughts went to Lindsey, and he swung around. "Where's . . ."

"I'm here." Lindsey sat atop his horse, guiding the animal forward with her legs.

Will closed the distance between them, and she threw her leg over the front of the saddle and slid into his arms. He held her for what seemed an eternity, but it wasn't nearly long enough.

She felt good. She felt whole. She felt alive.

Finally, he backed up enough to look into her eyes without releasing his hold on her. "You're crazy, woman. What if that horse had thrown you? Or kept on running?"

"He's *your* horse, Will. I knew he wouldn't do either. Besides"—she devastated him with a smile—"you're the one who sent him running with that slap on the rump."

"Yeah, well . . ." Will brushed a damp curl away from her cheek. "We all have our moments of stupidity."

She laughed lightly. "It worked, didn't it?"

"Yeah." Her smile was infectious. "But only because you're one hell of a rider."

"Did you ever doubt it?"

"Not for a moment." He started to kiss her and then remembered Eric. Turning toward the other man, who held Ray and Gus at gunpoint, Will said, "By the way, what the hell took you so long?"

Eric shrugged. "He was too close to Lindsey. I couldn't get a clean shot. When I saw my chance, I took it."

"Well, you took your sweet time." Will feigned annoyance, though he'd never felt more grateful to anyone in his life. Eric had given Will his chance, distracting Gus for the moment it took Will to make his move. "And what was that with the shots at his feet? I thought you were supposed to be a crack shot?"

Eric met his gaze and grinned. "I didn't want to spoil your fun. You were dying to get your hands on him."

Will laughed abruptly, knowing he owed this man.

"If you two are done congratulating each other," Lindsey said, turning her bound hands toward Will, "would you mind?"

Will smiled sheepishly and started untying her, while Eric moved the two criminals a safe distance away. Once Lindsey was free, Will turned her back around, his thoughts once again centered on her welfare.

"Are you okay?" he asked.

"I'm tired, hungry, and cold." She smiled. "But I'm okay."

He pulled her close. "Did they . . . hurt you?" He couldn't bring himself to voice his real concern.

She drew back and looked into his eyes. "Would it matter if they had?"

He realized his mistake instantly and hauled her back into his arms. "God, no." He would never hold such a thing against her. "I just needed to know whether I was going to turn them over to the sheriff dead or alive."

Again, Lindsey laughed, a sound that went straight to his heart. "It's okay," she said. "We can take them in alive."

Chapter Fourteen

Lindsey lingered over her coffee.

She'd finished breakfast at least fifteen minutes earlier, but she was in no hurry to head outside and start work. Even the early morning sunlight spilling through her kitchen window failed to brighten her mood.

It had been three days since Gus and Ray had been taken into custody. Three days with no word from Will.

She knew she shouldn't expect anything more from him. After all, he'd saved her life. What more could she ask? Yet, she wanted more. So much more. When he'd brought her home after turning Gus and Ray over to the authorities, he'd kissed her—a long, sweet kiss filled with promises. Or at least, that's what she'd thought.

She hadn't seen him since.

Granted, there had been a lot going on. Besides the hours they'd both spent with the sheriff going over the events of the kidnapping and rescue, she'd been busy with her brother's legal problems. She'd hired a lawyer, and Stuart had been released on his own recognizance. Then there had been the cleanup after the fire. She also knew Will had his own place to take care of. A spread the size of the Lazy W didn't run itself. So it wasn't like either of them were just sitting around. Still . . .

"Lindsey, you better come see this."

She looked up at one of the hired hands standing in the kitchen doorway. "What is it?"

"Uh . . ." He hesitated and glanced behind him before answering, "You better come see for yourself."

Curious, Lindsey followed him out into the yard.

Coming up the drive was a long line of cars and trucks, stretched out as far as the eye could see. She stood dumbfounded as the first truck stopped in front of her.

Will climbed out. "Morning, Lindsey."

Her heart leaped at the sight of him. "Good morning." She didn't know what else to say.

She watched as vehicle after vehicle pulled up behind Will and parked wherever they could find a space. People poured from the cars and trucks—folks from town and from the neighboring ranches. She'd known most of them all her life, but there were a few new faces as well.

"What's going on?" she asked Will.

Before he could answer, Dory Westman pushed in front of him, carrying a huge pot. "Morning, Lindsey, mind if I use your kitchen?"

"Uh, sure." What else was she going to say when one of the county's leading ladies showed up on her doorstep at the crack of dawn? "Go ahead."

Dory headed for the house and a stream of women followed, each toting some platter or tray and nodding their good-mornings to Lindsey as they walked into her house.

Lindsey turned back to Will, who grinned and shoved his hat to the back of his head. "Don't mind Dory," he said.

"She was supposed to wait until we asked your permission."

"My permission? Will . . ." She stepped closer to him, ready to strangle him if he didn't start explaining himself.

"Well, it's like this—"

"Hey, Lindsey." Eric walked up beside Will and gave Lindsey a huge smile. "How you doing?"

"Eric," Will said. "You're interrupting. I was just going to explain why we're here."

"Oh, sorry. I figured you'd already got to that part."

"Not yet," Will replied before turning back to Lindsey. "It's like this," he said again. "We're here for a couple of reasons. First,"—he glanced around at the group of men who'd gathered behind him—"we thought you might need help building a new barn."

Stunned, it took her a moment to respond. "You mean like a . . ." She was afraid to say the word in case she'd misunderstood. "A barn raising?"

"Yep, an old-fashioned barn raising," Eric answered, but smiled his apologies when Will threw him a warning glance.

"I can't believe it," Lindsey said, not sure what to say. "I mean, how did you . . ." Then, thinking of all these men and the work they'd left at their own places, she said, "I can't ask that of any of you."

"You didn't ask, Lindsey," Will said. "We're all here because we want to help. Isn't that right?"

A series of agreements came from the men standing around. Lindsey felt the tears sting her eyes. All these people were here for her. And Will . . . She knew it had been Will's doing. And again, she didn't know what to say.

"Just say thank you," Will said, as if reading her mind.

She smiled. "Thank you. And yes, please, we need the help. My men are at your disposal."

Eric nudged Will in the side. "Tell her the rest."

"The rest?" Lindsey turned to Will.

"The second reason we're here." Will smiled and took a step toward her, and something tightened in Lindsey's chest. "We came for a wedding."

Lindsey stepped back. "A wedding?"

"Will you marry me, Lindsey?"

She shook her head, though in truth she would have rather thrown her arms around him. She was so tired of fighting her feelings for this man. And of being alone. "We've been over this," she said, though she couldn't put any conviction in her words.

Will pulled out a piece of paper and handed it to her. "Maybe this will clear things up a bit."

"What is it?"

"Read it."

Hesitantly, Lindsey looked over the document. It was a legal document, a deed to be exact. Looking back at Will, she said, "I don't understand."

"That paper makes you sole owner of the Silver Creek Ranch. The entire property, including what used to be the Claxton Ranch."

Again, she just looked at him.

"I bought out Stuart's share in the ranch, and had the whole thing put into your name."

"Can you do that?"

"I already did. Now, there's no question of why I want to marry you. I love you. You're all that matters."

She looked around at the sea of expectant faces.

"We even brought a preacher," Eric said.

"I don't know what to say."

Will stepped forward and took her hand. "Say yes."

She looked up into his dark, sexy eyes and saw her answer. Will loved her. When had it happened? Or had it always been there, and she'd just been blind?

"We were both blind," Will said. "You've always been my best friend, my love. It just took me a while to see it."

Lindsey felt her resistance melting away. "You mean it." It wasn't a question. "You really want to marry me. Be my husband."

Will pulled her into his arms. "For the rest of our lives."

— THE END —

Note from Pat

I hope you enjoyed Loving Lindsey and will try another book in the series. Also, please take a moment and leave a brief review of the book to help spread the word. Thank you.

Just follow the link. Loving Lindsey

About the Author

Patricia Keelyn writes contemporary romance and romantic suspense.

She's published twelve novels and several short stories independently and for the three major publishes, including: Ballantine, Bantam, and Harlequin. Her last three books were hardcover suspense novels released under the pseudonym Patricia Lewin.

Pat also teaches writing workshops and classes in various formats and length around the country at at her coral Community College.

For more information or updates:
Pat's Website
Pat's Reader List

Join and follow Pat on: Facebook, Goodreads, and Bookbub.

 facebook.com/PatriciaKeelyn

Patricia Keelyn Books

THE PROTECTORS
Collection
PATRICIA KEELYN

Loving Lindsey

Rough Around the Edges

Running for Cover

Nobody's Hero

Becca and the Beast

A
Mother's Heart
Collection

Keeping Katie

Once A Wife

Where The Heart Is

Box Set

Patricia Lewin Books

Blind Run Collection

Blind Run

Blind Run Short Stories

Hide

Away

Erin Baker Series

Out of Reach

Out of Time

Standalone Short Stories

Helen Told Me